MORRIS AUTOMATED INFORMATION NETWORK

0 1091 06

W9-AUW-251

Parsippany-Troy Hills Library
Main Library
449 Halsey RD
Parsippany NJ 07054
973-887-5150

WITHDRAWN

WITHDRAWN

WITHDRAWN

AUG 3 1 2018

WITHDRAWN

Lucky Luna

Diana López

SCHOLASTIC PRESS / NEW YORK

Copyright © 2018 by Diana López

All rights reserved. Published by Scholastic Press, an imprint of
Scholastic Inc., *Publishers since 1920*. SCHOLASTIC, SCHOLASTIC PRESS,
and associated logos are trademarks and/or registered trademarks of
Scholastic Inc.

The publisher does not have any control over and does not assume any
responsibility for author or third-party websites or their content.

No part of this publication may be reproduced, stored in a retrieval
system, or transmitted in any form or by any means, electronic,
mechanical, photocopying, recording, or otherwise, without written
permission of the publisher. For information regarding permission, write
to Scholastic Inc., Attention: Permissions Department,
557 Broadway, New York, NY 10012.

This book is a work of fiction. Names, characters, places, and incidents
are either the product of the author's imagination or are used fictitiously,
and any resemblance to actual persons, living or dead, business
establishments, events, or locales is entirely coincidental.

Names: López, Diana, author.
Title: Lucky Luna / Diana López.
Description: First edition. | New York, NY : Scholastic Press, 2018. |
Summary: Fifth grader Luna Ramos has a great many cousins, mostly
on her father's side, but one of them, Claudia, is a source of constant
annoyance; their current feud begins when Luna is punished for locking
Claudia in the restroom at another cousin's quinceañera—but when
there's a bullying situation at school, Luna realizes that, despite their
disagreements, cousins have to stand up for each other.
Identifiers: LCCN 2017049157 | ISBN 9781338232738 (hardcover) |
ISBN 9781338232745 (pbk.)
Subjects: LCSH: Cousins—Juvenile fiction. | Hispanic American
families—Juvenile fiction. | Practical jokes—Juvenile fiction. |
Bullying—Juvenile fiction. | CYAC: Cousins—Fiction. | Hispanic
Americans—Fiction. | Family life—Fiction. | Practical jokes—
Fiction. | Bullying—Fiction.
Classification: LCC PZ7.L876352 Lu 2018 | DDC 813.6 [Fic]—dc23
LC record available at https://lccn.loc.gov/2017049157

10 9 8 7 6 5 4 3 2 1   18 19 20 21 22

Printed in the U.S.A.   23
First edition, September 2018

Book design by Baily Crawford

To Aunt Beatrice, in loving memory

La prima

My cousin Mirasol is having a quinceañera, a celebration for her fifteenth birthday. All of my primas on Dad's side are here, and *most* of them are dancing in beautiful purple dresses because they're damas, which is the same thing as saying "ladies in a royal court." I'm *not* a dama, so I don't get to wear a purple dress. I'm not dancing, and neither is Mabel, the most loyal friend in the world.

Mabel and I sit right by the dance floor. Everybody else is twirling and doing fancy steps in front of us. I can't help tapping my feet, and when I glance over, Mabel's tapping her feet, too. Then my parents pass right in front of us.

"Come on, Lucky Luna!" Mom says. "You can't sit there all night." My dad lifts his arm, and she spins under it, three times. I'm dizzy just watching.

"Why don't you want to dance?" Mabel asks.

I cross my arms. "I'm protesting because I'm not in the royal court. I have too many primas, and they took all the spots."

"How many cousins do you have anyway?"

I shrug. Then I get a great idea. "Maybe I should count them."

We stand on our chairs to see the entire dance floor. *One, two, three*—I'm pointing as I count—*four, five . . .*

Oh no! Some of my primas moved.

I start over. *One, two, three, four, five, six . . .*

Wait a minute. I can't remember which cousins I've already counted.

One, two, three, four, five, six, seven . . .

It's impossible. Even if I could count the primas here tonight, it wouldn't cover everyone. I'm here with my dad's side of the family, but I have a whole other group from my mom's side. I'm never with *all* my primas in the same place at the same time because we'd have to rent a football stadium to make that happen.

"I give up!" I say to Mabel. "My cousins keep moving, and lots of them are wearing purple dresses. It's like counting goldfish in a pond. Have you ever tried to count goldfish in a pond?"

Mabel shakes her head. "No, but I *did* try counting the stars one night. I had to give up because there are just so many of them. At first, I felt sad, but then I realized that every star is a wish. Can you imagine it? A sky of countless wishes?"

"No," I answer. "But I *can* imagine a sky of countless primas." As I say this, I picture all of my cousins' faces peering down at me and I shudder.

"I wish *I* had a bunch of girl cousins," Mabel says. "I have a few, but they're in the Philippines. This is how many times I've seen them." She curls her fingers and makes a zero.

"Better than seeing them every day."

"Why?"

"Because every time I'm in trouble, a cousin is involved."

Mabel scratches her head, which means she's thinking. Then she says, "But—and before I say anything else, promise you won't get mad?"

I put my hand over my heart. "I promise."

"Well," Mabel continues, "you get in trouble at school—not *all* the time but sometimes—and your cousins aren't even there."

She has a good point but only because she doesn't have all the facts. "It's still their fault," I explain. "When I forget my homework, it's because a prima came over to my house and distracted me. When I *don't* forget my homework but get the answers wrong, it's because a prima helped me. And when I get in trouble for other stuff, it's because a prima planted a bad idea in my head."

Mabel laughs.

"What's so funny?"

"Oh, nothing. I just imagined a bunch of leaves coming out of your ears when you said 'planted.'"

I laugh, too, but then I get back to the topic. "So there you have it. Too many primas is a bad-luck thing, especially when your cousin is having a quinceañera and she doesn't ask you to be in her royal court."

This is the first time Mabel's been to a quinceañera, so I tell her that only fourteen girls (one for each year of the birthday girl's life) get to be damas. First, Mirasol asked a few friends. The rest of the slots went to primas, but *I* didn't get picked. My dad has six siblings, and his oldest sister, Tía Margo, has five daughters, one after the other. We call them the "quins," short for "quintuplets." Two are already twentysomething, but the others are still teenagers. And that's not counting my dad's other siblings and all of *their* daughters. Most are older than me, so they get to have all the fun.

The worst part is not being in the official photograph! A few weeks ago, Mirasol and her damas wore their fancy dresses and went to the fountains in front of the art museum for a photo shoot with a professional photographer. When they gave a copy of the picture to my abuela, she framed and hung it in her hallway next to other photos of fancy events. I'm not in a single one, so it's like I don't exist at all.

I moped around after seeing that picture, and no one could cheer me up. Then Mirasol invited me to her house a few days later. She apologized and explained that she chose by age, starting with the oldest, because she didn't want to pick favorites. Then she painted my fingernails. She even drew little palm trees on my ring fingers with a glittery dot for the coconut. It was hard to be sad after that. Still, she should have picked the *nicest* cousins instead of oldest because *that* would have been *me* for sure.

I glance around the dance hall and search for Mirasol. She's posing for pictures beneath un arco covered in purple flowers. Her beautiful white dress has lots of ruffles and lace, and she has a tiara sparkling in her blond hair. Her hair's not *really* blond, but she bleaches it. My other primas surround her—Estrella, who runs all the time, Nancy, who does weird science experiments in her garage, and even Kimberly, whose favorite class is shop. They're all wearing the same purple gown because you're supposed to match when you're part of a royal court.

Mabel puts a hand on my shoulder. "I just thought of a good-luck thing," she says.

"Really? Something better than standing in my cousin's quinceañera, wearing a beautiful purple dress, and being in the official picture?"

"Yes." She points at my head. "At least you get to wear a cowboy hat, and you love hats more than anything in the world."

I glance up and smile. I've got a beautiful cowboy hat. It's white like my cowboy boots, and it has a yellow band to match my yellow dress. "That's right," I say. "Damas can't wear cowboy hats."

Just then, my parents pass us again. "Start dancing!" Mom orders.

I can only sigh.

"What's wrong?" Mabel asks.

"How can I go out there with a cowboy hat when they aren't playing country music?"

Now it's Mabel's turn to sigh.

Next they play "Bésame," a Spanish love song, and my parents dance real slow. Then they play an oldie but goodie song, "Rockin' Robin" by Michael Jackson. For this song, Abuela carries my brother, Alex, to the floor. He's two. She swings him around, and his laughter is louder than the music. Then they play pop tunes—for over twenty minutes!

I start to think that my night can't get any worse, but then I see *her*—Claudia—my prima with the giant nose. She's in the fifth grade just like me. I hate how she bosses me around and always brags about stuff—like getting a ribbon for perfect attendance or winning a poster contest or being in the photo on Abuela's wall. She's one month older than me, so she got to be in the royal court even though *I* don't show off or boss people around.

Here comes Claudia with her mean, angry face. She marches right up to Mabel and me, and then she points at my boots. "This is a dance, *not* a rodeo. You're supposed to wear cowboy boots with jeans, not with dresses."

"I can wear whatever I want, *whenever* I want," I say.

"Would you wear a bathing suit to church?" she asks. "Would you wear pajamas to school?"

I want to say that I would happily do both of those things, but then I imagine the nuns scolding me and my teachers sending me to the principal's office.

"I thought not," Claudia says, because she knows I'm stumped. "It's a dumb idea to wear cowboy boots with dresses." She marches away before I can talk back.

I narrow my eyes as I watch her leave. I'm just so mad!

Claudia sits at a table with her mother and Abuela. They start talking, probably in Spanish and probably about me. When Claudia turns and glances back at me, my aunt and abuela glance back, too. They are *definitely* talking about me! One thing I hate is gossip, and in my family, there's a lot. You can't say or do anything without everybody else knowing. I can only hope that Abuela is scolding Claudia for saying mean things. But wait! She doesn't look mad. She looks concerned. She's taking Claudia's hand!

"I feel so betrayed," I say.

"Why?" Mabel asks.

I shrug, too frustrated to explain.

A few minutes later, Claudia leaves the table, weaves her way through the dancers on the floor, and then flings open a swing door to the dance hall's foyer.

"Let's follow my cousin," I tell Mabel.

When we get to the foyer, Claudia is nowhere around. There are only four places she could be—the parking lot, the men's restroom, the ladies' restroom, or the bridal room.

"Logic dictates that Claudia is in the ladies' restroom," I say, pointing to the door.

My dad's a Trekkie, which means he loves to watch *Star Trek*, so he's always saying things like "Make it so," "Beam me up, Scotty," and "Logic dictates." I can't help it. I've got these phrases in my head, too.

Mabel and I step inside, but Claudia's not there. So Mabel stoops over and peeks beneath the bathroom stalls. "Looks empty," she says.

"Claudia?" I call out. "Claudia, I know you're in here." Nothing but silence. Maybe she's standing on a toilet. "Are you standing on a toilet?" More silence, but to make sure she isn't hiding, I open every single stall. All empty.

"I bet she went outside," Mabel offers.

"Or the dressing room," I say. "And if she went to the dressing room, she's in big, big trouble. My aunt Sandra told us to stay out because she doesn't want us touching Mirasol's beauty products."

We head to the dressing room, which is really *three* rooms: first a small room with a sofa; then a room with a giant mirror, a vanity full of makeup, and a counter with a straightening iron and almost ten different hair products; and then the last door, another restroom. I had peeked in earlier. It's fancy, with lavender air freshener, a picture of flowers, and extra space for when brides wear puffy dresses. The restroom door is closed, but I can hear someone inside. Aha!

I signal to Mabel, putting a finger to my lips so she'll be quiet. Then we tiptoe back to the room with the sofa.

"I'm going to lock Claudia in the restroom," I tell Mabel.

"Why? You're just going to make her mad."

"That's the point," I say. "She makes *me* mad, so I should make *her* mad, too."

"Or we could forget about it and go back to the dance hall instead," Mabel suggests.

"Claudia thinks she's too good for the ladies' room," I go on. "If she wants the fancy restroom all to herself, then she can have it. Besides, there's no end to how mean she can be. If you ask me, leaving her in a fancy restroom for a few minutes is letting her off too easy."

I tiptoe back to the dressing room, but Mabel doesn't follow. When I give her a questioning look, she says, "I'll wait here." So I go in alone, and as soon as I enter, I hear the toilet flushing. I need to be quick or I'll miss my moment. Luckily, there's a wooden chair nearby. I grab it and anchor it beneath the doorknob.

Almost immediately, I see the doorknob turning, but of course, the door doesn't budge.

"Hey," Claudia calls out. "Who's out there?"

I hear Claudia push against the door, and I imagine her shoulder slamming into it. I can't help giggling.

"Is that you, Luna?" Claudia says. "You better open the door right now!"

Instead of opening the door, I run out before I'm caught. This time Mabel follows me, all the way to the dance hall.

"You're going to get in trouble," she warns.

She's probably right. I think about turning back, but then I remember the time Claudia put a dead roach in my underwear drawer and how she said that if I ate snacks in my room, I was going to have a lot more roaches, *live* ones, because of the crumbs.

So I might get in trouble for locking her in the rest-room, but at least I'll get even, too.

Olvidar

Back at the dance hall, I'm ready to forget about Claudia being stuck in the restroom—but Mabel doesn't let me.

"Okay," she says. "Claudia's been in the restroom for a whole minute. Now it's time to let her out."

"Absolutely not."

"I already told you, Luna. You're going to get in so much trouble."

"Why would I get in trouble? No one saw me do it, so unless Claudia has X-ray vision and can see through doors, there's no way she can prove it was me."

"But don't you feel sorry for her?" Mabel asks. "If I were locked in the restroom, I'd worry about being stuck forever with nowhere to sit but an uncomfortable toilet seat." She frowns. "What happens when you run out of toilet paper? How horrible!"

"Stop!" I say. "You're getting carried away. She won't be in there forever. Just for a few more minutes."

We hear a new tune from the DJ.

"Country music!" I cheer. And sure enough, they're playing "Boot Scootin' Boogie," my favorite line dance!

"Let's go dance to this song," I say, "and then we'll come back for Claudia."

"Promise?"

"Yes, I promise. We'll be back in five minutes."

Mabel glances at the bridal room and then at the dance floor. "Okay. Five minutes," she says.

So we run to the floor and get in line between Abuela and Dad. We swing our right legs forward and tap our heels. We swing our left feet backward and tap our toes. We do a whole bunch of other steps before bringing our feet together and clapping. And then we repeat the whole thing. And I'm doing it better than everybody because I have boots, and the "Boot Scootin' Boogie" is all about boots. That's why it's called "*Boot* Scootin'" in the first place.

When the song ends, Mabel heads toward the foyer, but I grab her wrist. "One more," I say, because the DJ's playing another country tune, "Cotton-Eyed Joe," Texas-style. This is my favorite dance because it's the only time I get to say a bad word. We get in a line, skip forward a few paces, then hop backward while kicking and singing "What you say? Bull****!"

When the song ends, Mabel says, "We should get Claudia now. You promised. More than once."

"Are you kidding? She's probably been out for ten minutes. I bet a dozen people have used that bathroom already."

Mabel looks around. "I don't see her, do you?"

Truth is, they're still playing country music, and I want to take advantage of my boots. "Come on," I say, grabbing Mabel's hand.

"Yes, but what about your cousin?"

"She's fine." And sure enough, Claudia *is* fine because there she is, stepping into the dance hall with Nancy, her older sister, behind her. I point. "Look!"

Mabel sees her and gives a big sigh of relief. Then we hear the opening notes for the Chicken Dance. We love this dance because we get to act silly, and seeing my abuela act like a chicken cracks us up.

Now that Claudia's out of the restroom, Mabel stops worrying. For the next song, my dad asks me to dance, and while I'm circling the floor with him, Mabel's circling the floor with Alex. They aren't really dancing, more like holding hands and skipping, but nobody cares. Lots of people make up their own steps.

Then the country playlist ends, so Mabel starts to head back to our seats. At the same time, Claudia and her mother, Tía Nena, start marching toward me. If I'm at my table, they'll talk to me for sure. Claudia can't prove anything, but that won't stop her from blaming me for the restroom incident. I need to hide, and right now, the best place is on the crowded floor.

"Let's keep dancing," I tell Mabel. "They're playing 'Y.M.C.A.' and one of the guys in the band wore a cowboy hat and boots, just like me."

We make our way to the middle and act like cheerleaders making Y.M.C.A. letters with our arms. When the song ends, I stay on the floor even though there's no more country music. The more I dance, the more I forget about Claudia and about not being a dama in Mirasol's royal court.

I'm about to give the night an A-plus, but then Mom spots me and calls me over. She's with Claudia, my prima Kimberly, and Tía Nena.

When I reach them, Mom says, "Is it true that you locked Claudia in the restroom?"

I know lying is bad, but sometimes it's good. Like when your aunt Priscilla wants your opinion about her new hair color—and it's the same color as the powder on Cheetos, which looks ugly when it gets all over your hands and even uglier when it's all over your head—but if you admit this, you'll get in trouble and hurt your dear aunt's feelings. This is what goes through my mind when Mom asks me if I locked Claudia in the restroom. That's why I lie, but lying to Mom isn't easy. When I'm nervous, I fast-talk, so a bunch of words spill out and most of them spill out on their own.

"Why would I lock her in the restroom? I'm too busy having fun. Didn't you tell me to dance? Well, I danced, so I've been following your orders all night. Ask Dad. And Abuela. They were dancing with me. Think about it. When would I have time to lock someone in the restroom? Besides, I've got wimpy arms. I can't lift a shoebox, so how could I possibly lift a whole chair?"

Mom crosses her arms, a really bad sign. "Who said anything about a chair?"

Uh-oh. I am so busted.

Right then, Mom starts yelling at me. Mabel hangs her head even though *she's* not the one in trouble.

"What's wrong with you?" Mom says. "Claudia's your cousin. You're supposed to be nice to her. You aren't supposed to be locking her in restrooms."

"She started it," I say. "*She's* the one who put a dead roach in my underwear drawer."

Claudia jumps in. "*You're* the one who snipped my ukulele strings."

"Only after you took a picture of me sleeping with my mouth open and posted it on Instagram!"

"But it got twenty-seven likes."

"And a comment that said I drooled!"

"Girls!" Mom shouts, and at the same time, Tía Nena says, "¡Cállense!"

But Claudia isn't finished. "I was in that restroom for

a very long time. I thought someone was trying to kidnap me, and I was scared for my life!"

What a liar! "You weren't scared for your life," I say. "You knew it was me the whole time."

"But I wasn't *sure* it was you because you just left me there without saying a word. I thought I was going to be kidnapped *forever*!" With that, she throws herself into her mother's arms. She really knows how to be dramatic. Kimberly is behind them, and she rolls her eyes. At least *one* person in my family knows that Claudia likes to exaggerate.

Now Tía Nena is yelling at me, but I don't know what she's saying since she's yelling in Spanish, and my parents never speak Spanish to me. It takes forever for my aunt to stop and catch her breath, but when she does, my mom takes over again.

"I could try giving you extra chores," she tells me. "Or stopping your allowance or grounding you. But none of those things seems to work. So . . ." She thinks a moment. If she had a see-through skull, I'd probably see a lot of sparks going off in her brain.

"So?" I say, wincing.

"So no hats for a whole month."

I gasp. Everyone knows I love hats. Everyone knows I *need* them, and since they aren't against my school's dress code, I wear them every day.

"But—" I try.

"No 'buts,'" she says. "Now apologize to Claudia."

When I don't speak, she nudges me.

"I'm sorry," I mumble.

But Mom wants more. "And?"

"And I promise not to do it again."

"And?"

"And I promise to be nice to you from now on."

She finally seems satisfied. "Well," she says, "you're going to have plenty of chances to be nice because Claudia's transferring to your school."

I do a double take. "What? When?"

"Monday."

I turn to Claudia. "Did you know about this?"

She nods and smiles, but it's not a nice smile. She looks like an alligator about to snap its jaws, and I can't help feeling like she's snapping those jaws around me.

El chisme

My family has enough gossip for its own twenty-four-hour news network—but instead of CNN or Fox News, we'd call it the Chisme Channel. When my prima Josie wanted to break up with her boyfriend because he couldn't stop talking about weird facts like how much sweat your feet produce (a pint per day!) or how many burgers McDonald's sells (seventy-five per second!), my primas and I heard about it before he did. We also heard about Estrella winning her first track race, only by the time *I* got the story, Estrella was going to the Olympics because of the world record she broke. But that's not what happened at all. She broke a *school* record, and it was a lot slower than the slowest person who ever ran in the Olympics. And even though *I* didn't say anything, my primas heard about the time in second grade when I flushed a hat with a fluffy ball on top and flooded the girls' restroom, and the time in third grade when I landed in mud after jumping out the classroom window because I didn't know the fire alarm was fake and didn't think walking in a straight line down a long hall was the best way to avoid flames and smoke inhalation, and the time in fourth grade when I went to the principal's office for drawing a picture of my teacher's face, including a few nose hairs. I wasn't making fun of her—honest! I was being realistic by paying attention to detail, but that didn't matter. Every single prima heard about it, and they couldn't stop laughing even after I explained that my teacher no longer had nose hairs because she plucked them out after seeing the picture, which proves that I actually did her a favor.

So I'm absolutely positive that there's got to be chisme about the quinceañera last night. Maybe something embarrassing happened to one of my primas or one of them got busted for kissing a boy.

I open my laptop to Skype with Paloma. She's already in middle school, two years older than me, but she talks to me as if *I'm* in middle school, too. That's why I like her so much.

"Prima!" she says when her face appears on my screen.

"Prima!" I say back.

She doesn't waste time. She gets right to the gossip, but instead of talking about somebody else, she's talking about me!

"What a crazy night, right?" she begins. "I can't

believe you locked Claudia in the closet at the quinceañera."

"Restroom," I correct.

"And that she was in there for three whole hours!"

"Thirty minutes, tops."

"And now you can't wear hats ever again for your whole entire life!"

"For a month," I say. "But it *feels* like a lifetime."

In the background, I spot a guitar, a music stand, and Paloma's mariachi outfit hanging from a hook on her closet door. It looks like it just came back from the dry cleaner's. The purple dress she wore last night is crumpled on the bed.

Then Mirasol comes into the room, cell phone against her ear. She's wearing wrinkled pajamas. Her hair's a tangled mess, and her eyes are smudged with mascara. I guess being a quinceañera queen really wore her out.

"Who are you talking to?" Paloma asks her sister.

"Celeste," Mirasol replies. Our prima Celeste is the same age as Mirasol, so they're *always* talking.

Mirasol peers into the computer to look at me. Just like Paloma, she gets right to the gossip. "I can't believe I didn't notice the excitement. Celeste says that you locked Claudia in the trunk of a car last night."

"No," I answer, laughing. "Where would she get a crazy idea like that?"

Mirasol shrugs. "Something about kidnapping her."

"Kidnap!" Then I remember. "Oh, Claudia was exaggerating, trying to get me in more trouble. All I did was lock her in the restroom."

She repeats this to Celeste. Then she plops onto Paloma's bed, right on top of the crumpled dress, and starts talking about her boyfriend. Paloma rolls her eyes and turns the screen. Instead of her mariachi outfit in the background, I now see a dresser with a pile of books and board games.

"Did you hear that Claudia got transferred to my school?" I say, and while Paloma's nodding, I add, "Why is she coming to my school? Doesn't she go to Sacred Heart? Isn't she always bragging about going to a private school?"

"I heard she talked back to one of the nuns," Paloma says.

"Really? What did she say?"

"I don't know. Probably something about the homework assignments. It's only the second week of school, and she was already complaining."

"So she got kicked out because she didn't want to do her homework?" I shake my head the way Mom shakes her head when *I* don't do *my* homework.

"That's not why she's transferring," Mirasol interrupts, her voice offscreen.

Paloma turns toward her sister to hear more. I look in the same direction even though I can't see Mirasol.

"Uncle Freddy bought a boat," she says, "so they don't have money for private school. There was a big fight about it. Tía Nena told him that a good *education* is more important than a good *vacation*, but Uncle Freddy said he's always wanted a boat and that Claudia could go to school for free like everybody else." She stops talking, but I hear her mumbling "uh-huh" and "ooh." Then she goes on. "Celeste says that Tía Nena was so mad she threw a box of Popeyes fried chicken at the boat!" She starts laughing. "I wonder if it was spicy or mild." She's still talking, but her voice fades away.

"She's gone," Paloma says. "I hate the way she just waltzes in and out of my room all the time. No privacy."

"You think it's true?" I ask. "About the boat and the fried chicken?"

"Naw. Celeste probably made that up because Claudia tattled on her. She found Celeste kissing her boyfriend in the parking lot at the dance last night."

I gasp, pretending to be shocked even though I'm not.

"Now Celeste is grounded," Paloma says. "She can't wear hats for a whole month."

"Really? She can't wear hats, either?"

"Oh, wait." Paloma taps her chin. "*You're* the one who can't wear hats. I guess Celeste got some other kind of punishment. Anyway, she's mad, and she vowed to never talk to Claudia again." Paloma shakes her head and then continues. "I'm sure Claudia talked back to one of the nuns and got kicked out of Sacred Heart. It makes more sense. She's probably using the boat as an excuse because she doesn't want anyone to know she got in trouble. You know how she likes to show off."

"Tell me about it," I say, remembering how Claudia bragged about being a dama because she knew that *I* wanted to be one, too.

"Did I tell you about the time . . . ?" Paloma begins. She's got ten—maybe twenty!—examples of Claudia acting like she's better than everyone else. I say, "She didn't!" and "No way!" and "That's ridiculous!" and "Who does she think she is?"

We talk for almost an hour. I'm smiling and laughing, but when we hang up, I spot Dad in the doorway, arms crossed.

"Were you eavesdropping?" I ask.

Instead of answering with a yes or no, he says, "If you can't say something nice, then don't say anything at all."

Great, I think. *Claudia's not here, but she's still getting me in trouble.*

El Domingo

Today's Sunday, so Monday's not far behind. And that's the day Claudia transfers to my school. She can't go to my school. She just *can't*!

School is my chance to take a break from my family. Some of my primas go to the same high school, and all they do is spy on one another. If Claudia goes to *my* school, she'll spy, too. She'll tell her mom everything I do and her mom will tell my mom and my mom will tell me. And by the time I hear about it, I'll be in so much trouble—especially because Claudia's going to focus on all the bad stuff I do and conveniently forget to mention the good stuff, even though I'm mostly good!

I need to find Mom. Maybe she can convince Claudia to find another elementary. First, I look in Alex's room, and then I remember that he's at Cole Park with Dad. I look in the kitchen, but Mom's not washing dishes or slicing veggies or baking pies or anything. Then I look in the sewing room, where she does arts and crafts. She's not there, either. I peek into the laundry room, the garage, and finally the backyard. That's when I find her. She's sweeping up leaves from the patio.

"Why is Claudia transferring to my school?" I ask. "Is it because Uncle Freddy and Tía Nena had to claim bankruptcy after buying a yacht and throwing fried chicken and mashed potatoes at it?"

Mom laughs. "You have a wild imagination."

"So they're not bankrupt?"

"No."

"But we've only been in school for two weeks. Did Claudia talk back to the nuns? Is that why she's transferring?"

"No, she didn't do anything like that. She's transferring because her school only has a choir. There aren't any clubs or sports. She's really good at kickball and wants more practice so she can be in the Little Miss Kickball League next spring."

"But why Woodlawn?" I cry out. "Can't she go somewhere else?"

"Nope. She lives in the Woodlawn district."

"But she should stay at Sacred Heart. She's going to miss her old friends. It's hard to make friends when you go to a new school."

Mom uses a dustpan to scoop leaves into a trash bag. When she finishes, she says, "*You'll* be there and you're her prima, which automatically makes you her friend."

"But friends and cousins are not the same thing!"

"That's right," Mom says. "Friends come and go, but cousins are forever." She scoops up another pile of leaves.

"If that's true, then I'm going to be *miserable* forever."

Mom sighs. I can tell she's getting impatient. Why doesn't she understand?

I try to explain. "Friends hang out with you because they *want* to, not because they *have* to. I could list a hundred reasons why friends are better than cousins."

"Is that right?" Mom says, putting away the gardening tools. "You listed one reason. Why don't you give me the other ninety-nine?"

"Okay," I say, but nothing else comes out—not because there aren't any other reasons but because my mind goes blank when I'm put on the spot. "Well, let me see."

I twirl a strand of hair around my finger. Meanwhile, Mom waits.

After a few minutes, she says, "Don't you like playing volleyball when we go to the beach?"

I nod.

"There wouldn't be enough people for a team without your primas, right?"

I have to nod again.

"And who bought raffle tickets when you were selling them for your school?"

"My primas," I admit.

"That's right. And your primas are always giving you the books and hats and games they don't use anymore."

"Hand-me-downs," I say.

"*Gifts,*" she says back to me, and then she goes on. "Who teaches you dance routines and cookie recipes? Who invites you to parties? Who cheered for you when you played Villager Number Two in your school's production of *The Pied Piper*?"

Primas, primas, primas! They're the answer to *everything*. And, yes, some of my primas are nice and fun and interesting, but others? Others are bossy, annoying, and mean. They're a real mixed bag of pan dulces—some flaky, others dense, some sweet, others tart.

"Okay," I say, giving up. "But I still don't think primas are better than friends." And I walk off before she can list more reasons.

So Mom is no help. She thinks Claudia being at my school is like winning a raffle for a trip to Las Vegas and then winning $1,000 from a slot machine. If Mom can't help, then maybe Abuela can. I decide to run to her house. She lives across the street, so I go there all the time. They say old people are wise, and it's true. My abuela is also a great listener. She always lets me talk about my problems.

"Abuela!" I call through the screen door. She unhooks the latch and waves me in. Then she points to the rocking chair, so I take a seat and start rocking. Meanwhile, Abuela and her cat, Gato, get comfy on the couch.

"I've got terrible news!" I'm yelling because of the creaky rocking chair and because I'm upset. "Claudia is transferring to my school!"

"Ya lo sé," Abuela says. "Qué bueno."

"It is *not* bueno," I tell her. "It's horrible. It's the most horrible thing in the world!"

Abuela pets Gato, and he starts to purr. He seems so peaceful. I wish I felt that way, too.

"She'll spy on me," I go on. "She'll tell my parents everything. Like when I get bad grades and when I forget about rules and when I break rules even before they're invented." I'm rocking super fast now. "She'll tell my *teachers* everything, too. Like when I don't do my homework or when I say something bad—even when the bad thing is true—like the time I talked about how Coach was getting fat. I thought she was maybe eating too many Big Macs. I didn't know she was pregnant. It was an honest mistake. But Claudia doesn't care about my *intentions*. All she wants is to get me in trouble. And I'm going to be in trouble *all the time* if we go to the same school!"

I tell Abuela about the time Claudia put jalapeño slices in my sandwich when I wasn't looking and about the time she borrowed my T-shirt and got it full of stains from the juicy hot dog she was eating. She said she did it by accident, but I know it was on purpose. And . . . okay . . . maybe I stole the shoelaces from her favorite pair of Skechers, but only because she lost my library book! I had to pay a fee or never go to the library again. And whenever Mom calls me Lucky Luna, Claudia whispers, "There are *two* kinds of luck—the good kind and the bad kind," and then she twitches her nose and says, "Guess what kind you are."

"I must be the bad kind," I tell Abuela, "because Claudia at my school is a very bad-luck thing."

By now, I'm not rocking so fast. I'm slowing down. All that rocking and talking has made me tired.

"What am I going to do?" I cry. "I can't let her meet my friends. She'll embarrass me!"

Abuela sits quietly for a while. It's because she's wise, and wise people never blurt out answers. They think first. After a long time, Abuela nods and says, "La sangre es más espesa que el agua."

When I hear Spanish, it sounds something like this, "Let's go, blah, blah, blah" or "blah, blah, cookies, blah,

blah." So when Abuela gives me her wise advice, I hear, "Blah, blah, blah, water." I try my best to translate, and only one thing makes sense. She's telling me I should drink water when I'm mad about Claudia.

"Good idea," I say as I head to Abuela's kitchen for a drink. I gulp down a whole glass of water. When I return to the living room, Abuela is still on the couch with Gato.

"Thanks," I say. "I feel a lot better now."

She smiles. "Qué bueno."

La luna

Luna means moon, and it's also my name. You might think it's weird to be named after something that hangs in the sky. But lots of people in my family are named after things that hang in the sky.

My prima Estrella's name means "star." Mirasol's name means "look at the sun," and Celeste's name means "sky," plain and simple. Then there's Paloma, whose name is Spanish for "dove." Maybe doves don't hang in the sky like the stars and the moon, but they fly in it. So "Paloma" is a sky name, too. I don't know what Claudia's name means in Spanish, but it sounds a lot like "cloud" when you say it. So that's what I think of when I say her name. Clouds. Clouds that look like faces with giant noses.

My parents didn't name me Luna on purpose. They did it by accident. This is because my mother is very superstitious.

When you're superstitious, all kinds of things are bad luck. Some things are bad luck because Mom says so—like leaving dirty clothes on the floor or chewing your nails or scaring your brother in the middle of the night. Other things are bad luck because *everybody* says so—like walking under a ladder or spilling salt or opening an umbrella inside the house.

The bad-luck thing that gave me my name goes something like this: If a pregnant lady looks at the moon during a lunar eclipse, her child will be born with a giant birthmark that covers half the face.

My mother knew about this bad-luck thing. As soon as she got pregnant, all her sisters warned her. "Don't look at the moon!"

Guess what! She looked at the moon. "I couldn't help it," she tells me. "The moon was just so beautiful."

Of course, she felt horrible when she looked at it. She didn't want her child to have a giant birthmark, so she begged the moon to forgive her. But she didn't really beg the moon. She really begged the *rabbit* in the moon.

Yes! There's a rabbit in the moon. In the United States, people see a man in the moon, but in Mexico, they see a rabbit. I live in the US, but I live in the "Sparkling City by the Sea," Corpus Christi, which is near the bottom of Texas. A long time ago, Corpus Christi used to be part of Mexico, so we see some things the Mexican way.

Here's how to see the rabbit. Look at the dark spots on a full moon. The rabbit's body is curled over the edge. There's a giant spot where his head belongs and two long ears pointing to the center.

So Mom asked the rabbit in the moon to erase the birthmark from my face. And the rabbit listened! I was born with ten fingers, ten toes, and a beautiful, birthmark-free face. Mom was so grateful that she named me Luna to thank the moon. And because the bad-luck thing didn't happen, she decided to call me Lucky Luna even though it's not my official name.

I'm grateful to the moon, too, but I'm more grateful to the rabbit. John-John McAllister, a boy in school, carries a purple rabbit's foot for good luck. I guess he's superstitious just like my mom, but instead of bad-luck things, he believes in good-luck things. I want to believe in good-luck things, too. That's why I want a pet rabbit. If a rabbit's foot is good luck, then a *whole* rabbit must be *terrific* luck.

If I had a living good-luck rabbit, Claudia would not be transferring to my school. And if I had a living good-luck rabbit, I wouldn't be grounded from wearing hats. Truth is, I'd rather be sent to my room without supper for a whole month. I'd rather use a toothbrush to scrub the toilet or dust away spiderwebs beneath the kitchen sink. I'd rather write "I will not lock my primas in the restroom" 5,649 times till my hand is cramping and the skin on my fingers is rubbed raw. In other words, I'd rather have any other punishment because not wearing hats is the worst thing I can imagine.

Here's why: I've been wearing hats for as long as I can remember. My little brother is almost two years old and still doesn't have much hair. Lots of babies are born bald, and I was born bald, too. Mom put cute bonnets on my head to let people know I was a girl. In all my baby pictures, I'm wearing a bonnet. So I've been wearing hats my whole life, and when I'm *not* wearing one, I feel like I'm not wearing anything at all. I feel *naked*, and it's very embarrassing to be naked in front of everybody.

Plus, I don't have normal hair. My hair is wild and curly, which doesn't bother me at all. What bothers me is something *else* that makes my hair stand out.

When she was pregnant, Mom looked at the moon, remember? And she asked the rabbit in the moon to protect me from birthmarks, but there are so many kinds—port wine stains, strawberry marks, and Mongolian spots, the bluish mark that Mabel had when she was born that for her went away as she grew older. But I've got another type of birthmark—a streak of white hair!

That's why I'm all stressed out. First, today's the day Claudia goes to my school, and second, I can't wear hats because I'm grounded. If I were truly lucky, I'd have a stomachache or a broken leg or a dentist appointment so I wouldn't have to go to school. But I feel a hundred percent okay. How *unlucky* is that?

I have no choice. I go to the bathroom to wash up, and when I turn on the sink, I remember to calm down by drinking water. It works! Plus, it helps me realize a very important detail about Mom. She doesn't have a good memory!

For example, when she tells me she's going to the grocery store, I always ask for a Snickers bar but she brings me apples instead, or when she asks what I want for my birthday, I always say a rabbit but she buys me books. Once, when I was still reading picture books, she *almost* got it right because she gave me *The Tale of Peter Rabbit,* and even though I was grateful, it wasn't what I asked for. "I don't want *stories* about rabbits! I want a *real live* rabbit!" I told her, and she replied, "Well, rabbits are a lot of responsibility."

Usually, Mom's memory problems are bad news for me, but this *has* to be the day that luck wins out. After all, my name isn't Lucky Luna for nothing. So I stand before my bookcase, which is really a "hatcase" because instead of books, it's full of hats. I have all kinds—knit caps (the plain kind *and* the kind with bunny or puppy ears), cowboy hats, big floppy hats, a fedora that used to belong to my grandpa, a Santa Claus hat, and lots of baseball caps. I have every color, too. I study the hats and fall into what Dad calls "a state of analysis paralysis," which basically means I can't make up my mind. I finally pick something. Since I'm wearing a blue shirt, I decide to wear a blue baseball cap. It has a picture of a shark because it's from the Texas State Aquarium.

Then I hear Mom's voice from the kitchen. "Lucky Luna, make it quick!"

She sounds impatient. What if she's still mad at me for locking Claudia in the restroom? Will I get in *more* trouble if I wear my hat?

I stand before the mirror. The hat looks great, but I take it off to see what I look like. Then I put it back on. Then I take it off and put it on, back and forth about five times. Which is worse—wearing the hat or *not* wearing it?

If I wear my hat, I'll get in trouble, but if I *don't* wear it, everyone will know about my poliosis, which is what you call my streak of white hair. It's not contagious, but it sure does sound like a terrible disease.

La cocina

I go to the kitchen once I'm dressed. I've got my cap on, hoping Mom won't notice, and I'm looking forward to my favorite breakfast, orange juice and Pop-Tarts. I can already smell a strawberry Pop-Tart in the toaster, so I'm very happy when I walk in. But then right next to Alex is Claudia. She's sitting in my seat, drinking my orange juice, and eating *my* Pop-Tart. Looking at her makes me think of Goldilocks and how she made herself at home when the bears weren't around.

I'm not a bear, but I sure feel like growling. I know it's rude, but I point at Claudia anyway. "What is *she* doing here?"

Mom smiles at me. "Tía Nena and I had a wonderful idea," she says. "It's hard to be the new kid at school, so Claudia's going to ride the bus with you."

"But *Mabel's* my bus friend."

"And I'm sure she'll be more than happy to welcome your prima," Mom says.

Claudia's mouth is full of Pop-Tart, so she doesn't say anything. And I'm glad because if she could talk, she'd probably brag again.

When I sit down, Mom places two Pop-Tarts in front of me, but they aren't strawberry! They're blueberry, the kind with no frosting.

"Where are the strawberry Pop-Tarts?" I say.

Mom frowns a little. "I'm sorry, mija, but Claudia had the last ones." At this, Claudia smiles at me. She just loves to see me suffer.

I am so mad! But then I remember my abuela's wise advice. I go to the sink and pour a glass of water. I drink the whole thing, and when I'm finished, I don't feel as mad anymore.

"You sure are thirsty," Mom says.

And I say, "Can I take a water bottle to school? I have a feeling I'm going to be thirsty all day."

"Of course," Mom says, grabbing a bottle from the pantry and handing it to me.

Soon it's time to go to the bus stop, but before we head out the door, Mom tells me to take off my cap. Of course she'd remember! Her memory loss never works in my favor.

"No hats for a whole month," she reminds me.

"I promise to take it off when I get to school," I try.

Mom holds out her hand because she wants me to give her the cap.

"But my hair," I say.

She takes the cap off my head and gently combs my hair with her fingers. "Your hair is beautiful."

This is why they say that love is blind, because it ignores the ugly parts—and the ugly part of me is that streak of white hair.

I don't show that I'm embarrassed, because Claudia's here. So instead of focusing on my hair, I talk about something else as we wait for the bus. "Is it true your dad bought a boat?" I ask.

"Yes. Who told you?"

"Celeste told Mirasol and Mirasol told me."

"You were talking to Mirasol?" She seems jealous.

"*And* Paloma."

"When?"

"Yesterday."

Claudia bites her lower lip. Now I *know* she's jealous.

"And I talked to Estrella and Kimberly, too." I didn't *technically* talk to them, but I'm not really lying since I heard what they said because Paloma and Mirasol told me.

"How about Marina?" Claudia asks.

I shake my head. I already told a white lie about Estrella and Kimberly, and I don't want to stretch the truth too much.

She scoffs. "I would have talked to them, too, but I was busy having fun on my dad's new boat. You can't use phones when you're in the middle of the ocean. No reception." She glances at me, narrows her eyes. "I guess you wouldn't know since you don't have a boat."

"Yes, I do," I say. "My family has a kayak."

"Kayaks don't count," she replies. "*Our* new boat has a motor. *You* have to use oars."

Before I snap back, the bus arrives. As we climb in, I think about our kayak and how it flips over when we take it to the beach. It's not a bad-luck thing because flipping over is fun. With my life jacket, I float right up. Sometimes I *make* myself fall off, but if I tell Claudia that I do it on purpose, she'll think I'm lying when I'd be telling the truth.

The bus driver doesn't say anything when we step in, not even "Buenos días." Saying "good morning" would be nice, but our bus driver *isn't* nice. He's really grouchy. He says, "Stay in your seats!" or "Don't throw things out the windows!" or "¡Cállate!" If it ends in an exclamation point, he says it. And he has this deep vertical line between his eyebrows when he's mad. Lots of people have this line. My dad calls it "the line of consternation," and the older you get, the deeper it gets, so the bus driver must be very old.

As soon as Claudia and I pass by the driver, I say,

"Mabel is my bus partner, so I'm going to sit with her. You need to find your own place to sit."

And she says, "Good. Because I didn't want to sit with you in the first place."

So I find Mabel and sit beside her. Claudia is right behind me like a tagalong. As she walks through the aisle, some kids hold their noses, and one of them says, "Skunk." I glance at Claudia. She doesn't seem happy, but she doesn't say anything because she's the new kid. All the new kids are singled out until they aren't new anymore. It takes about two weeks to stop being new. If Claudia gets mad at the kids holding their noses, she'll be singled out even more.

Under my breath, I tell Mabel, "They're making fun of my prima's giant nose."

"Why do you think she has a giant nose?"

"Because she *does*. Just look at it."

Mabel peeks over the seat. Claudia has found a place three rows behind. She's all by herself, which is fine with me. Mabel waves, and Claudia waves back. Then my prima opens a book, but I'm not fooled. She isn't reading. She's trying to hide.

"I guess her nose is a *little* big," Mabel says, which doesn't make sense. Things are either little *or* big. If you say something is a "little big," that's like saying it's normal.

"You are too nice," I tell Mabel, because she's always looking at the bright side of things even when the bright side is darker than a tunnel with no flashlights or lanterns to light the way.

I'm not the only one who thinks my prima's nose is big because the kids on the bus keep making jokes about it. They are so immature.

I should be mad for my prima's sake, but I'm not. Serves her right for being so mean all the time. For example . . . after I snipped the strings on her ukulele, Mom made me write an apology. It took a long time because I was zero percent sorry for what I did. Saying "I'm sorry" when you're *not* is hard. When I gave Claudia the letter, she didn't even say thank you. Instead, she marked it up with red ink because I misspelled words and put commas in the wrong places. She even wrote an "F" at the top, just like a mean teacher. So don't blame me for being happy when the kids on the bus make fun of a nose that looks like a giant hot dog bun in the middle of my prima's face!

La abuela

We get to school and walk into the building. Then my bad-luck day gets even worse. Some kids see me and say, "Hi, Grandma," and some other kids point and laugh at me. I don't have a comeback because my white streak of hair *does* make me look like an old person even without the wrinkled skin and the deep line of consternation.

"I can't believe it," I whisper to Mabel. "Without a hat, I look old."

"Just ignore them," Mabel says, but it's hard because *everyone's* staring at me, and then a little kid says, "How come your hair's white?"

Instead of sounding mean, he sounds curious, so I say, "It's a birthmark. It's called poliosis, and I'm not the only person in the world to have white hair like this."

He just blinks a few times and runs away. I guess he's never talked to a fifth grader before.

I hate being singled out. Do I really have to deal with this for a whole month?

Thankfully, I don't have to walk the halls alone because Mabel and I are going to the same class, but before we go to our room, she pulls me over to the Club Board, a bulletin board with sign-up sheets for different activities.

"Finally!" she says, because it took a few weeks for the clubs to get started.

Right away, she signs up for Newsletter and then hands me the pen. I shake my head. I helped with the newsletter last year, but instead of being fun, it felt like work. We had to research, attend extra events, interview people, write paragraphs, and proofread. No way. Not for me. But it's absolutely perfect for Mabel because she wants to be a journalist someday. She actually *likes* doing the extra work. I don't know what I want to be, but I *do* know that it won't require writing. Maybe I can raise rabbits.

"Are you sure you don't want to sign up for the newsletter?" she asks. "Are you really going to make me join by myself?"

"You won't be by yourself." I point at the sheet. We recognize all the names.

Just then, Claudia squeezes between us. "Is this where you sign up for the Little Miss Kickball League and other clubs?"

I roll my eyes. The answer is so obvious. Luckily, I don't have to answer because Mabel takes over. She points out different clubs and the schedule for their meetings. She also shows Claudia lists of supplies for each club and the parent permission forms. Then the five-minute bell rings, so we head to class.

We're in room 112, which isn't far, but today, I can't get there fast enough. We pass the teachers' lounge and the nurse's office. We pass room 108, with the tank that has goldfish, and then we pass room 110, with the hamster. Finally, we get to room 112, *our* room. We have a lizard. I wish we had a rabbit because I really need some good luck, especially when I realize that Claudia's being a tagalong again. She's probably taking notes about kids calling me Grandma so she can tell my mom, *her* mom, and all my primas.

"Quit following me," I tell her.

"I'm not. I'm going to my class."

"Well, so am I," I say as I step through the door. When Claudia steps through, too, I get so mad! What else can I do but grab my water bottle for a huge gulp?

Claudia shows me a paper and points at it. "Looks like we're in the same room." Sure enough, she's in 112, too.

"Why would they put you in *my* class?" I say.

She shrugs. "I don't know. I'm supposed to be with the smart people."

See how mean she is? If I were a dog, I would growl. But I'm not. I'm a girl with a wise abuela, so I take her advice and drink more water. The bottle is almost empty now. That's how much I needed in order to calm down.

I take one last swallow before speaking again. "Well, you can't sit next to me. Mabel is my classroom friend and John-John McAllister is my *other* classroom friend, and I don't have room for any more friends in the classroom."

"That's fine," she says. "I don't want to sit next to you anyway."

With that, she marches to the teacher's desk, and when she gets there, she smiles and talks with a sweet voice, so *of course* Mr. Cruz says, "I'm so glad to meet you."

I shrug it off and head to my seat. Mabel and John-John are already there, and John-John is shaking his head. "I can't believe they're *still* talking about what happened last week!"

He's talking about the day he threw up. He's always thinking about the zombie apocalypse, who's going to live and who's going to get "zombified." Of course, *he's* going to live because he knows survival tactics. At least, that's what he says. He actually brags about it, so last week, some boys dared him to eat a worm during recess. It was an earthworm straight from the dirt, and it was still wriggling when John-John put it in his mouth. He chewed a few times and swallowed. He even stuck out his tongue to prove it. Most of the kids were disgusted, but *I* was impressed. Everyone agreed that John-John had a good chance of surviving the zombie apocalypse because after the stores run out of food, he can just dig for worms, and worms are quite nutritious. That's why birds eat them. Unfortunately, all that nutrition ended up on the classroom floor, because as soon as we got back, John-John upchucked the worm *and* the grilled cheese sandwich he'd eaten for lunch.

"I don't smell worm-and-cheese vomit anymore," Mabel says.

"Neither do I," I add.

John-John shakes his head. "Then why do they think the room stinks?"

Mabel and I shrug, but maybe they're still making jokes about my prima's big nose.

The bell rings, and Mr. Cruz introduces Claudia to the whole class. When he says that she's my cousin, I want to disappear. I wish I had a blanket to put over my head.

I'm grateful when the morning announcements come on, so everyone can forget that Claudia and I are related. As soon as we hear "Please rise," we all stand up and say, "I pledge allegiance to the flag of the United States of America." Then the principal talks about a PTA meeting. And then I really, really, *really* have to pee because of all the water I've been drinking.

So I raise my hand for the restroom pass. Mr. Cruz says, "Why don't you take Claudia with you? That way, you can show her where the restroom is. And then you can show her the library, cafeteria, and playground."

I do not want Claudia to tag along, but I need the hall pass so I can go to the restroom before I have an accident. What can I do? I don't even have time to think about it. I nod, grab the pass, and rush out the door. Claudia follows. I don't talk to her because I need to go to the restroom *right now*! Lucky for me, it's across the hall. I get there just in time.

When I step out of the stall, Claudia is standing by the row of sinks, and I have a very bad thought that jolts me like a nightmare. Now that everyone knows Claudia and I are related, they're going to lump us together. We'll be a duo like Batman and Robin, but instead of heroes, we'll be weirdos.

After I wash my hands, we step into the hall. I don't walk anywhere. Instead, I point. "The cafeteria is down that hall. The library is over there, and the playground and gym are in the back."

"Aren't you going to show me?" Claudia asks.

"I just did."

"But aren't you going to walk me over?"

"Can't," I say as I head back to class. "Mr. Cruz doesn't like us to be away too long."

I race into the room, and since it takes Claudia a few

seconds to catch up, we aren't exactly together. And later in the afternoon, we aren't together during recess or lunch or music hall because I rush to each location. Poor Mabel has to jog to keep up.

"Why are you in such a hurry?" she asks, out of breath.

"Because."

"That isn't an answer," she says. Then she takes a guess. "You're trying to run away from Claudia."

"No, I'm not."

Mabel stops, forcing me to stop, too. She crosses her arms, raises an eyebrow, and studies me. "I've been your friend since first grade." That's Mabel-talk for "you're lying." She lets this sink in before saying, "It can't hurt to be nice to your cousin. You should try."

"How can I be nice to her when she's so mean to me?" Mabel still has her arms crossed and an eyebrow raised, so I go on. "This morning she kept bragging about a fancy boat her dad bought and then she made fun of my dad's kayak."

"She did?"

"She said it doesn't have a motor and it looks like a bright yellow banana." I'm exaggerating, but that's definitely something Claudia would say.

Mabel just giggles. "But it *doesn't* have a motor," she says, "and it *does* look like a banana."

I can't believe it! Mabel thinks it's okay for Claudia to

brag about her boat? I give a few more details to change her mind, and before I know it, I'm getting carried away. "She said it's going to sink in the middle of the ocean and that I'll have to float there with my life jacket and hope the Coast Guard happens to find me because I won't be able to call 911 since there's no cell phone reception, and if I'm out there too long, I'm going to start hallucinating and then the sharks are going to attack. No one will ever know what happened to me and all because I was on a giant banana instead of a fancy boat."

"Well," Mabel says, "don't take the kayak to the middle of the ocean. Stay close to land so people can see you waving your arms."

"That's not the point, Mabel. I'm trying to explain why I want to stay away from my cousin. Who wants to hear about getting eaten by sharks?"

She thinks about it. "I see what you mean," she says, but she doesn't sound convinced.

She race-walks by my side anyway because friends are loyal even when they don't agree with you. And that's *another* reason why they are better than cousins.

¿Dónde está?

When I step into my house after school, Mom asks, "Where's Claudia?"

A few seconds pass, and before I can make up an answer, Claudia walks in. "Luna ran away from me all day," she announces.

"I did not," I say.

"Did too. You were *literally* running." She fans herself with a folder to show how tired she is from chasing me.

"I did *not* run. I walked at a normal pace. It's not my fault you're so slow."

Claudia turns to my mom. "She even pushed aside some kids to get away from me, and at lunch, she said the empty seat at her table was being saved, so I had to sit with strangers."

"It *was* being saved," I say.

"No, it wasn't. I kept looking. No one ever sat there."

"Is this true?" Mom asks me.

"No," I say. "Claudia just wants me to get in trouble. I can't help it if no one wants to be her friend." And before Mom can tell me that you don't need friends when you have so many primas, I run to my room, slam the door, grab a pillow, and *throw* it because I left my water in the kitchen and don't know how else to calm down.

I don't come out till Claudia leaves. I find Alex in the living room. He's sitting beneath the coffee table, so I stoop down. "What are you doing under here?"

He barks. Then he sticks out his tongue and starts panting. He likes to act like different animals.

"So you're a dog today, huh?"

He barks again. I reach over to pat his head.

A few minutes later, Dad comes home. Most dads say "How was your day?" but mine turns into a *Star Trek* captain and says, "Status report."

"It was a terrible day," I begin. "The kids kept saying 'Hi, Grandma!' or 'Where's your cane?' or 'Show us your dentures.'"

I repeat every insult I heard, plus a few extras, and to make sure he understands how upset I am, I try my hardest to cry. No tears come out, but I manage to frown and sniffle. Guess what! Instead of getting angry and calling the principal like a *normal* father, he smiles, snaps his fingers, and starts singing about being positive and forgetting the negative.

Then he repeats the song and starts dancing!

"Dad!" I say, because I want him to get serious. I know where some of the kids taunting me live, and I was thinking we could throw rotten eggs at their houses. "Dad!" I say again, but he's just singing and dancing. Alex comes out from beneath the table and starts spinning around. Mom comes in and dances, too!

Before I know it, I'm hooked. I can't let the whole family have fun without me, so I start dancing and singing along, even though I don't know what I'm saying. *"La, la, la, the positive. La, la, la, the negative."*

After a while, we all tire out, so Mom takes Alex to give him a bath while Dad gets comfy on his chair.

"I'm glad you feel better, mija," he says.

"I might feel better right now," I explain, "but it's not going to last, not as long as the kids can see the white streak in my hair. Can you tell Mom to let me wear hats again?"

"I'm afraid not," he says. "When it comes to discipline, we need to present a united front."

I hang down my head. "What am I going to do?" I sigh.

"I told you in that song," Dad says. "Focus on the good things, and try your best to ignore those kids. Eventually, they'll stop."

I can only shake my head. This is weak advice. Couldn't he give me some good comebacks instead?

I go to my room, and after a while, I come up with some positive things. First, everyone will forget about my hair when my hats return next month. Second, Claudia's getting teased, too, but unlike me, she'll be teased for the rest of her life because she'll *always* have a giant nose. There's no way to cover it up. There's plastic surgery, but it's only for the rich and famous. Claudia isn't rich *or* famous. Poor girl. Come to think of it, I kind of feel sorry for her.

Mabel says I should be nice to my prima, but I *am* nice. *She's* the one who's mean. But maybe it isn't her fault? Maybe she's mean because people make jokes about her nose. Maybe I should take Mabel's advice and treat my prima more like a friend.

La amiga

The next morning, I wake up in amiga mode. I'm going to pretend that Claudia is my friend, and I'm going to focus on the positive, even when she's getting on my nerves. So, when she's sitting in my chair for breakfast—this time with the last blueberry muffin, the one I was saving for myself—I smile and say, "Good morning, Claudia. Are you enjoying breakfast?"

Her mouth is full, so she takes a moment to swallow. Then she says, "Are you being sarcastic? I can't tell."

"No," I say in a pleasant voice.

"Oh . . . okay . . . well, then . . . I'm enjoying breakfast very much." She takes a giant bite. I can smell the delicious blueberries, and my stomach growls. If she were Prima Claudia instead of Amiga Claudia, I would yank the last half of the muffin and stuff it in my mouth before she could grab it back. Instead, I'm stuck with a dry piece of toast, and I tell myself that it's okay because friends make sacrifices for each other. Plus, I have water, which is good for calming nerves and for washing down things like toast with no butter or jelly or honey because my parents need to go to the grocery store.

We're about to leave when my mother says, "Lucky Luna, Tía Nena's going to get you after school today. You're going to spend a few hours at Claudia's house."

I glance at Claudia and she nods. I hate when she knows things before I do, but I remember my secret promise and pretend that she's a friend.

"Okay," I say, cheery. Then to Claudia, "Maybe you can show me your dad's new boat."

"It has a motor," she reminds me, "*and* a cabin. It goes so fast that it skips over the waves, and it never flips over like the kayak."

Instead of getting mad at the way she shows off, I imagine the cabin of her boat with a little kitchen and sleeping area. "I bet it's cool," I say. "Can't wait to see it."

She gets a suspicious look on her face. I can tell she wants to ask if I'm being sarcastic again, but she doesn't.

We head to the corner, and soon the bus arrives. When we step inside, some of the kids snicker. I can tell they want to make jokes about Claudia's nose, so I do what Dad calls a "preemptive strike," which means stopping enemies *before* they attack. I stand in the middle of the aisle and make an announcement. "If you can't say something nice, then don't say anything at all."

The first and second graders sink in their seats. The older kids roll their eyes, but they don't say anything, so that's okay.

I scoot beside Mabel.

"That was . . ." She searches for the word. "Brave." Then she quietly claps. "Good job of standing up for yourself."

"Myself *and* Claudia." I glance back. My prima's sitting three rows behind again. She doesn't notice me because she's reading. "Looks like she's still trying to hide behind a book. Can't blame her after those jokes about her nose."

"Hmmm . . ." Mabel mutters, thinking. "Remember that time your aunt colored her hair and turned it orange?"

"My aunt Priscilla? The one with hair that looked like Cheetos?"

Mabel nods. "Did you ever tell her about it?"

"No. Sometimes, it's better not to say anything, especially if it's embarrassing. It's like they say, 'What you don't know can't hurt you.'"

Mabel nods. "That's what I was thinking."

"Why are we talking about my aunt anyway? I thought we were talking about Claudia."

"We are. Sort of."

"Well, I'm taking your advice, Mabel. I'm going to treat Claudia like a friend. I'm going to ignore the zillion ways she gets on my nerves."

"Good," Mabel says. "I'll help you. Then we can all be friends, and the next time we have a class vote, she'll take our side."

Last week, we voted on whether to create a bulletin board about math or poetry. Mabel, John-John, and I wanted poetry, but we lost. So now our board has definitions for different shapes—the hexagon, octagon, and dodecahedron, which has twelve sides. Then we created dodecahedrons out of construction paper and hung them from the ceiling like Christmas balls. Mine's a little lopsided. Every time I see it, I think about how awesome my poetry would have been. I would have written the best poem with lots of rhymes and similes.

We bounce in our seats as the bus rolls over the speed bumps in the parking lot of our school. It squeals to a stop and the doors swoosh open. Mabel and I make our way down the aisle, waiting for Claudia to join us once we're outside. The three of us walk into the building and visit the Club Board. Claudia has decided to join kickball and Needle Beetles, which has its first meeting next Monday. She tells me I should learn needlecrafts, too, but poking my fingers and getting cross-eyed as I try to see the thread is not my idea of fun.

When we enter the class, Mabel and I introduce Claudia to a few more kids. At lunch, we invite her to sit at our table, and during art, we share our supplies. I'm being *super* nice. Even Mabel says so. But that doesn't mean Claudia's acting nice, too. She says, "Sacred Heart has more books in its library" and "Sacred Heart has better food" and "Sacred Heart has the Pledge of Allegiance *and* prayers for morning announcements." Nothing at Woodlawn is good enough.

Using a sweet voice, I say, "But at least Woodlawn has a lot of extracurricular activities. Isn't that why you came here in the first place?"

"Yes, but Sacred Heart has a choir."

"But that's *all* it has."

"True, but it's a very good choir. They travel all over the country. They're even singing at the University of Notre Dame next summer. That's in Indiana, in case you didn't know."

Ugh! Will she stop already? Every time she mentions Sacred Heart, I want to yell—*If it's so good over there, then just go back!* But I don't. I take a large gulp of water instead.

Friends don't yell at friends, I write in the margins of my worksheets. *Friends smile and nod happily. Sometimes friends drink lots of water.* Since I keep drinking water, I have to ask for the restroom pass— three times!

John-John notices. "Why do you keep going to the restroom? Do you have a stomachache?"

"No, I'm just drinking lots of water." I don't feel like explaining my abuela's advice. The day's almost over, and being nice and patient has worn me out. I glance at Mabel, hoping she'll help me out.

"Luna's staying hydrated," she says.

John-John nods. "That's good, but don't drink *all* the water. You should stash some for the zombie apocalypse. I've already got three gallons hidden in my closet. We won't have water, electricity, or Internet once the zombies take over. You should save some nonperishable food, too."

"Like cans of corn," Mabel suggests. "And pasta."

We keep talking about zombies until Mr. Cruz tells us to get back to work. Then the dismissal bell rings. Yay! It's time to go home. But I'm not going home. I'm going to Claudia's. Luckily, Mabel doesn't have to ride the bus by herself, because she has a newsletter meeting after school.

It takes forever for Tía Nena to reach us because there's a traffic jam in front of the school, but eventually her car arrives. A blast of cold air hits us when we enter.

Tía Nena says, "How was your day, girls?"

"Bleh," Claudia answers. "It was okay."

What! Didn't she notice how nice I'm being? I'm itching to say this out loud. Instead, I reach for my water bottle. It's empty. Suddenly, the blast of cold air feels like an oven of dry heat.

When we get to Claudia's house, I ask her to show me the boat. It's on a trailer in the backyard. I was expecting a yacht with a deck for sunbathing and enough seats for all the primas on my dad's side, but it has room for only three or four people. We climb in. It smells like rotten fish. It has a motor just like Claudia said but no canopy for shade. The vinyl on the seats has cracked.

"Hey!" I say. "This isn't a new boat. It looks used."

"Previously owned," Claudia corrects. "Maybe it's not *brand*-new, but it's new to my family."

I don't comment, even though I want to. Instead, I ask to see the cabin, and she points to a little door at the front of the boat. I open it and peer inside.

"This isn't a cabin," I say. "It's a cubbyhole. I thought you had a little kitchen and a place to sleep. You don't even have windows in here."

She rolls her eyes. "Whatever. You can go inside if you want."

I step into the dark creepy space. There are cushions on a bench that opens up for storage and a square plastic thing with a lid.

I grab my nose and pinch it. "Is that a toilet?"

"Yes," she says as if it's obvious.

"Does it flush?"

"No. It's a portable toilet. You have to empty it when you get back to land."

"That's gross!" I say.

"Not as gross as peeing in your pants."

She looks at me, and I look at her. Then we start laughing. We can't stop. For some reason, the portable toilet is the funniest thing in the world, especially when I imagine trying to pee in a rocking boat. Soon, we're holding our stomachs because we're laughing so hard.

We finally settle down, and I climb out of the cabin. "We should be explorers," I say, and she agrees. She even lets me play the part of Amerigo Vespucci while she plays Magellan, who was famous but not enough to have a whole continent named after him. Then we act out *Peter Pan*, and I get to be Captain Hook. After that, we switch to Pirates of the Caribbean. I play the hero, Jack Sparrow, and Claudia plays the villain, Davy Jones. He looks like an octopus with a bunch of tentacles on his face. The tentacles look like giant noses. I *think* this, but I don't *say* it.

"Let's be swashbucklers," Claudia says.

We grab sticks from the yard and pretend to swordfight. Our sticks clack against each other. We jump off the boat and climb back on, the whole time pretending to stab at each other and saying things like "You barnacle-faced fool!" and "You crusty landlubber!" Then I swipe at Claudia's "sword." She drops it and throws herself on the deck. I pretend to stab her chest. She grabs her heart and moans. Then she makes a big show of dying. She even kicks up her legs a few times and I almost forget how annoying she can be.

La semana

Claudia and I had fun on the boat, but it was a one-time thing because the rest of the week goes by and, every day, she gets on my nerves. She gets a perfect score on the spelling test, but I miss three words. She says, "I'm making higher grades than you." Then she finds my dodecahedron and tells me that everyone else's is perfect and symmetrical while mine is shaped like a pear. I try to explain that Earth is pear-shaped, too, but she just shakes her head.

During lunch, she sits at my table and makes fun of how I eat. "Salad dressing is for salads," she says, "not green beans." And "You're supposed to eat dessert *last*, not *first*."

Then she tattles to my parents. "Luna was talking in the library," she tells my mom. "Luna was passing notes during class," she tells my dad.

And she tattles to my teacher. "Luna doesn't have a rabbit, so there's no way a rabbit ate her homework" and "Luna didn't have emergency surgery on her pancreas so she had plenty of time to study."

I'm going to run out of excuses if she keeps tattling! This has got to be the most stressful *semana* of my life! I don't care how much fun I had on Claudia's boat.

Finally, it's Friday, which is a good-luck *and* a bad-luck day. Good, because of the weekend. Bad, because Mr. Cruz wants us to write Spanish skits today.

Spanish is my worst subject. I got an F on our first test last week. It was supposed to be a review of Spanish words we learned during fourth grade last year, but since I didn't practice over the summer, I failed. When Claudia found out, she bragged about being an A student.

I couldn't stand how high-and-mighty she was, so I said, "I *could* make straight A's if I wanted, but I like *all* the letters of the alphabet. I don't want the B's, C's, and F's to be left out. I feel sorry for them, so don't blame me for giving the other letters a chance to be on my tests. Some people believe in equal opportunity."

Claudia got the message. She might make straight A's, but I was a nicer person. And because she was jealous about how nice I am, she ran to my mom after school and said, "Did you know Luna failed a Spanish test on purpose?"

I wish my last name were Smith or Parker or Woo. No one expects a Smith or Parker or Woo to know Spanish. But my last name is Ramos. It's a very common name in Spain and Mexico, so lots of people with this name speak Spanish. In fact, my dad and abuela and half (but not all) of my cousins speak it. They think I can speak it, too, even though no one has ever taught me since my mom doesn't speak it, only my dad.

For our Spanish skits, Mr. Cruz hands out puppets and asks us to use vocabulary from our lessons. Puppets are kind of babyish, but we don't care. Anything's better than worksheets.

Mr. Cruz gives me a dog puppet. It's got floppy ears and a tongue that hangs out its mouth. Once we get our puppets, Mr. Cruz tells us to form groups. I join Mabel and John-John. He has the doctor puppet and she has the wizard.

I already have a great idea for our skit, but before I can share it, Claudia comes over. She's got the king puppet.

"Go find your own group," I tell her. "We already have our idea and it doesn't need a king," and to Mabel and John-John, I say, "Right?"

John-John looks away, not wanting to answer. Mabel says, "I don't know what our idea is yet, but I'm sure we can work in a king."

"We can't," I insist, giving her a stern look.

Claudia doesn't give up. "You got an F on your test, remember? You should let me help since I'm bilingual."

"We don't need your help," I say.

"Are you sure? I'm trying to be nice."

Is she crazy? She is everything *but* nice. "No, you're not," I say. "You're just showing off again because you think you're better than me."

"I *am* better than you, especially when it comes to Spanish."

If I were a rattlesnake, I'd strike her with my venomous fangs, but I'm not, so I just glare at her instead.

She shrugs it off. "Don't blame me when you get another F," she says, walking away and joining a group that has a chef and a ballerina.

When I turn back to my group, Mabel and John-John look stunned.

"If she knows Spanish," Mabel says, "we should let her help us."

"Yeah," adds John-John. "You know our Spanish is a big problemo."

It's true. John-John doesn't know any Spanish and that "problemo" really ends with an A. His family came to the US from Ireland and even though they say "wee" instead of "small," it's still English. Mabel doesn't know Spanish, either. Her family is from the Philippines, and she says they speak Tagalog. Poor Mabel. She needs her dad to translate when she talks to her lola. At least, *I* can talk to *my* abuela without a translator—sort of.

Mabel thinks I'm lucky because I know a little bit of Spanish, which is better than knowing none at all. But I think I'm *unlucky* because knowing a little bit makes people think you know a lot. Plus, the Philippine islands are thousands of miles away, and it takes a whole day to get there, even on the fastest airplane. But Mexico is only three hours away, even in the slowest car. A bunch of signs in Corpus Christi are written in English and Spanish, but you never see signs in English and Tagalog. That's why no one expects her to speak her family's language, but *everyone* expects *me* to speak mine.

At least my mom understands because she can't speak Spanish, either. "I guess my brain only works in one direction," she told me once. "I can translate Spanish to English but not English to Spanish." I know *exactly* what she's talking about because I have a one-direction brain, too.

"Don't worry," I tell Mabel and John-John. "We know enough for today. Besides, I have the dog puppet, and dogs only know one word."

After I tell them the plan, we rehearse, and then it's time for our presentation. When the teacher calls on us, we go to the front of the class.

"First," I say to everyone, "I would like to introduce our characters." I point to John-John. "This is Dr. McAllister." He bows. Then I point to Mabel. "This is the Magnificent Wizard of Corpus Christi, the Sparkling City by the Sea." She bows. Then I hold up my dog puppet. "And this is Rover." I let everyone clap, and then we perform our skit.

```
Rover: Woof! Woof!

Dr. McAllister: ¿Estás enfermo?

Rover (nodding): Woof!

Magnificent Wizard: Él necesita
medicina.

(Dr. McAllister gives Rover medicine,
and Rover makes loud gulping sounds.)

Dr. McAllister: ¿Estás bien?

Rover (shaking head): Woof!

Dr. McAllister: Él necesita magia.
```

Magnificent Wizard (waving wand):
Abracadabra.

Dr. McAllister: ¿Estás bien?

Rover (nodding): Woof! Woof! Woof!

In case you don't know any Spanish, Rover is sick. First they try medicine, and when it doesn't work, they try magic.

I think it's a great skit even without the zombies John-John wanted to add. Everybody else thinks it's good, too. I can tell because they're clapping. The only not-clapping student is Claudia, but that's because she's jealous. Since 99.9 percent of the students like our skit, I'm confused when Mr. Cruz gives us our grades. John-John gets an A, Mabel gets a B, and I get a C.

How come I got a C? I can't stop thinking about it, so when it's time for lunch, I tell Mabel that I'm going to stay behind for a minute. I need to talk to Mr. Cruz alone because he made a mistake, and I wouldn't want to point it out when other people are around. That would be the same as singling him out, and you never want to single out a teacher. It's very disrespectful, and they'll never ever forget. Trust me, I know. I accidentally singled out my teachers in first, second, third, and fourth grades. Thank goodness, it doesn't take me long to learn a lesson. That's why I patiently wait for the last student to leave the room.

Then I say, "Mr. Cruz, you gave me a C on the Spanish skit instead of the A-plus that I deserve. I know it was an accident, so I'm not mad."

"Oh," he says, and I can tell he's embarrassed about his big mistake.

"You can go ahead and change the grade now." I point at his grade book because he's too old-fashioned to use a laptop. "If you wait too long, you might forget."

"No, I won't forget," he says, and then he stares at me a minute. "Here's the thing, Luna. The C isn't an accident. I gave you that grade because you didn't speak Spanish, and that's what the assignment was all about."

"But our *group* spoke Spanish, and I helped them write the skit."

"That's why I gave you some credit, but the purpose of the skits is to practice the Spanish out loud."

"But I had the dog puppet. Dogs don't talk. They just make sounds."

He sighs. I can tell I'm getting on his nerves a little. Then he says, "It's true that in the real world, dogs don't talk, but in the make-believe world, they do. Besides, dogs don't even say 'woof, woof, woof' in Spanish, they say 'guau, guau.' And since this was a Spanish assignment, all the characters have to speak that language. Those are the rules."

"But, Mr. Cruz," I say. "Spanish is my worst subject, and if I fail, I'm going to be in big, big trouble, and I'll never get a pet rabbit for as long as I live, and all I've ever wanted is a pet rabbit. Can't you give me an A-plus, just this one time? Or if not, then maybe a B?"

"I am not going to change your grade," he says. "You have to earn the A by studying and practicing." Then he gets an idea. "Your cousin Claudia speaks Spanish fluently. Why don't you ask her for help?"

Now it's *my* turn to sigh. "I can't ask her because we fight all the time. We might be cousins, but we're not friends even though I *tried* to be her friend. I tried real hard."

Mr. Cruz shakes his head. "I'm sorry to hear that." Then he thinks a moment. "Well, don't you have other cousins? Surely one of them knows Spanish, too."

"Hmm . . . " I mutter. "As a matter of fact, I *do* have other cousins—too many to count. And most of them are nicer and smarter than Claudia!" Before Mr. Cruz can say more, I run out the door. "Thanks, Mr. Cruz! You just gave me a great idea!"

Enojado

Since it's Friday, everyone is extra loud from the excitement of the weekend about to begin, so the grouchy bus driver gets angry and reminds us of the rules:

1. Don't throw things out the window.

2. Don't leave trash behind.

3. Stay in your seats.

4. Don't shout!

We don't have a seating arrangement for the bus like we do for the classroom, but once you pick the same spot for three days in a row, it becomes your official seat.

The first graders take the front rows because they want to be friends with the driver. The second graders get the middle rows, where the big humps for the tires are, so they have to sit all cramped, with their knees up against their chests. The rest of us sit everywhere else. Everyone knows that the best seats are in the back. They're far away from the grouchy driver. Plus, they bump around, and it's fun to get bumped around when you're going to school. They're also the only seats with the back windows, which means you can wave or make funny faces at the cars behind the bus. Most of the fifth graders sit there, but since Mabel gets motion sickness, we sit near the middle, where it doesn't bounce so much.

All week I've been telling Claudia to join the other fifth graders, but she's still three rows behind us, so now it's her official spot.

"She just wants to spy," I tell Mabel.

Claudia overhears. "I do not want to spy. I don't care what you say or what you do. You are not that interesting."

"Then mind your own business," I tell her.

She holds up her book. "I *am*."

"She's just pretending to read so she can eavesdrop," I say to Mabel. We glance back, and sure enough, Claudia's eyes are peeking over the top edge of her book. She's *watching* us. It's so creepy!

I whisper now. "We can't say any secrets because Claudia will hear and tell my mother."

And Mabel says, "What will we talk about, then? Almost everything we say is a secret—like how I secretly wish I could walk into landscape paintings and explore the meadows or forests. If only I could go behind the painted trees or inside the painted cottages."

I sigh. It's a very nice secret, and I'm sad we can't share daydreams without Claudia telling us we're crazy and then telling everyone else that I'm crazy and so is my best friend.

Mabel says, "I've got an idea. Let's play hand-clapping games instead."

We haven't played hand-clapping games since third grade, but since there's nothing better to do, I give her a thumbs-up. So we face each other and start clapping. Our favorite rhyme has always been "Miss Mary Mack."

"Miss Mary Mack, Mack, Mack

All dressed in black, black, black

With silver buttons, buttons, buttons

All down her back, back, back."

We like to change the words. We say she's dressed in red with buttons on her head, or dressed in blue with buttons on her shoe, or dressed in green with buttons on her jeans. We'd like to dress her in orange and purple, too, but those words are hard to rhyme.

I'm having a good time, but then I catch two girls giggling from a few rows back, across the aisle. They're in fourth grade, and since they rode the bus last year, too, I know their names—Janie and Carly.

"What's so funny?" I ask.

Janie says, "We came up with another verse. Want to hear it?"

"Sure," I say, thinking they wrote something that rhymes with orange or purple.

So they begin, clapping their hands as they sing.

"Miss Mary Mack, Mack, Mack

All dressed in pink, pink, pink

Because of how, how, how,

How much she stinks, stinks, stinks."

And here's what I learn when I hear them laughing. There are happy laughs like when you get tickled, but there are mean laughs, too. When Janie and Carly start laughing, it's the mean kind. It's because they're making fun of Claudia's big nose. It's because they turned our fun rhyme into an insult.

I glance back at my prima. She's dropped her book. She's staring at Carly and Janie with a deep line of consternation between her brows. I guess young people can get lines of consternation, too, if they're mad enough.

"Don't you like our rhyme?" Janie asks us.

I don't know what to say. I can't explain it, but I'm mad. I might not like Claudia, but she's *still* my cousin. Even though my other primas and I sometimes talk about her, it is *not* okay for *other* people who are *not* related to *also* talk because when they say things about Claudia, they're saying things about me, too. That's what being related is all about.

"Well? Do you like our rhyme?" Janie repeats, because I haven't said anything.

Mabel's the one who answers. "You can keep it. We already have enough verses." Then she turns forward in her seat, so I turn forward, too.

A long time ago, someone drew stick figures on the back of the seat in front of us. All of the figures have circles for heads, dots for eyes, and straight lines for arms and legs. All the figures look alike, so they probably never get teased. I can't stop staring at them and wishing that I lived in a stick-figure world where everybody looked the same.

I glance at Mabel. She's staring at the stick figures, too. Without talking about it, we've decided to stop playing our hand-clapping game. We might never play it again.

When the bus reaches our street, Claudia and I get off. I'm feeling sorry for her, so I can't think of anything to say. If I mention Carly and Janie's rhyme, she'll feel worse, but if I don't mention it, she'll *still* feel worse because she'll think I'm pretending nothing happened. There are win-win situations, but this situation is definitely lose-lose.

Luckily, Claudia speaks first. "I've only been at that school for one week, but I can already tell it's full of mean kids."

"Some of them are mean," I say, "but some are really nice." It's true. Mabel and John-John are nice. Plus, *I'm* a student there, too, and I'm one of the nicest people on the planet.

"They make fun of . . . of . . . of people," she goes on. I can tell she doesn't want to admit that *she's* the one getting teased. "They made jokes all week long."

I know she's secretly talking about her nose, but since I got teased, too, I agree with her. So I repeat what my dad says when people need to change their behavior. "Some of them need an attitude adjustment."

"*Major* attitude adjustment," she says. And that's it. We don't talk about it anymore.

I feel so relieved. When something bad happens, it sits on you like a giant sofa right on top of your chest, and you can't breathe or wriggle out. You're just stuck beneath that awful, bad thing. But now that giant, bad-news sofa is gone, so I can breathe and move around again.

We're almost to my house when Claudia asks a question. "What's your favorite color?"

"Green," I say, and I go on. "Some people think it's a scary color since witches and snakes are green, and also aliens who look like lizards and want to take over the planet. But a lot of *nice* things are green, like grass, trees, and apple-flavored lollipops."

Claudia nods. "Green's a good color, and apple-flavored lollipops are delicious."

I can't believe it. Claudia and I just agreed about three things—attitude adjustments, the color green, and apple lollipops. I really can't figure out my cousin. Most of the time, she's irritating, but sometimes . . . well . . . sometimes she's nice.

But her kindness never lasts long. When we get to my house, Claudia can't help it. She's more interested in being a spy.

"Luna's really struggling with Spanish," she tells my mom as soon as we walk in. "She totally messed up today."

"Is this true?" Mom asks.

"No. I did not mess up."

"I'm pretty sure you didn't get an A on that Spanish skit," Claudia says, "or a B." Then, to my mom, "I offered to help, but she wouldn't let me."

Mom says, "Why didn't you let Claudia help? She speaks Spanish all the time."

I'm silent. No matter what I say, it will be the wrong thing. When Claudia's around, I'm *always* wrong.

How could I *ever* think about being her friend, for even half a minute? It will *never* happen. We'll be enemies now and forever, through all eternity, till the end of our days and beyond.

"Well?" Mom has her hands on her hips now.

"Excuse me," I say. "I need a tall glass of water."

I head to the kitchen to drink some water. Alex is there, too. When our eyes meet, he raises his arms so I can lift him. I pick him up. He's getting so heavy, but it's the good kind of heavy. Not like a bad-news sofa at all.

We hear the doorbell. Alex scrambles down to see who it is. I follow. It's Claudia's mom. Good. I don't have to see my prima for the next two days and that makes me very, very happy.

As they're walking out, I hear Claudia say, "Can we go to Hobby Lobby so I can buy some yarn for the needlecrafts club?"

And Tía Nena says, "Sure. I need some things, too."

Then they leave. Even though Claudia is my bitter enemy, I *would* hang out with her if it meant going to Hobby Lobby. It's one of my favorite stores. If I hurry, I could try and catch them before they drive off. But then I think of choosing a kit for friendship bracelets or a paint-by-numbers set, and I hear Claudia's voice saying something like "That's a waste of money" or "That's an ugly picture" or "*My* arts-and-crafts project is better than yours."

Never mind, I think. *I'll just stay home instead.*

Ándale

Ándale means "hurry," and the next day, this is what Dad says as he peeks into my room. "¡Ándale! Get ready. We're going to Joe's for a fish fry."

Joe's my dad's brother, which means he's my uncle. He's also the father of three primos—Mirasol, Paloma, and Little Joe, who's four.

I grab a beige fishing hat. To make it more interesting, Dad had removed hooks from some old fishing lures so I could pin them along the brim for extra style. I love adding a personal touch to my hats.

I put it on and adjust it, making sure it hides most of my white streak. Then I head to the kitchen, and as soon as Mom sees me, she says, "Take it off."

"But it's Saturday, and I'm not going to school."

"You're grounded for a whole month, period. School days *and* weekends."

I sigh, take it off, and refuse to offer my help with the Tupperware containers she's filling with coleslaw and watermelon. Every meal with my aunts and uncles is a potluck because there are so many of us, and it's too much work for one family to provide all the food.

Just then, Abuela walks in with a giant bowl of banana pudding, the kind with vanilla wafers—delicious! She never knocks or rings the doorbell since she lives across the street. It's as if my house and her house are the same building but with a street right down the middle.

I give her a kiss and a hug, and then I sit on the floor next to Alex. He's playing with little cars, so I make *vroom, vroom* noises for him.

Abuela says, "¿Y, Claudia? ¿Cómo le fue la primera semana en la escuela?"

All I hear is "And, Claudia? Blah, blah, blah, week, blah, school?" I can tell she's asking a question, so I say, "Yes, Claudia started going to my school this week."

"I think she wants to know how it went," Mom explains.

"Oh," I say. Then, "It was awful. Lots of kids made fun of her."

"Qué triste," Abuela says, and I know this means "how sad."

Mom frowns. "I hope you stood up for her."

I look down because I don't want to admit that the

only time I stood up for Claudia was when I made an announcement on the bus, and it only worked for one morning. Even when I started to feel sorry for her, I didn't tell the kids to stop making jokes or report them to the teacher.

"You're being very quiet," Mom says. "Did you let the other kids tease your prima?"

I nod, but then I say, "I tried to stop them, but there are lots of kids and only *one* of me. There's no way I could stop them all by myself." Mom sighs. I can tell she's disappointed. "If I talk back to the bullies," I go on, "they'll pick on me even worse because they're still making fun of my hair since you won't let me wear hats. If I start wearing hats again, then they'll stop making fun of me, and if they stop making fun of me, then all my problems will go away and I'll have energy to help Claudia. So you see? The answer is letting me wear hats again."

Mom says, "I'm not budging. You're still grounded. Besides, you have beautiful hair. You shouldn't care what those other kids think. They won't be around forever, but Claudia will *always* be around because she's your prima." She pauses a moment and then says, "Primas are for life."

Abuela nods. "Es la verdad."

"In fact," Mom says, "why don't you invite Claudia to the fish fry? We can pick her up on the way."

Is she serious? I want to shout "No way!" but if I do, I'll get in trouble. How can I convince Mom that inviting Claudia is a bad idea? I need to give her a reason, and the reason can't be "Claudia gets on my nerves."

So I say, "That's a great idea, Mom, but . . ."

"But what?"

"I need to study, and Paloma already promised to teach me Spanish."

I haven't exactly asked Paloma for help, but I'm sure she'll say yes when I do. I'm stretching the truth a little, but it's for a good cause.

"If Claudia's there," I go on, "I might get distracted from my lesson, and you know how much I need to practice. Paloma's going to help me make flash cards with Spanish words on one side and definitions on the other."

"Really?" Mom seems doubtful, so I nod with excitement. I *almost* cross my heart, but I stop myself because you're not supposed to cross your heart for lies no matter how small. If you do, terrible things will happen. Lightning will strike and set fire to the land. Giant swarms of locusts and bees will darken the skies and blisters will form all over your body.

"Okay for today," Mom says, "but next time, we'll go pick her up."

When we get to Uncle Joe's, Paloma's not there. She's at a rehearsal for her mariachi band.

"She'll be home soon," Aunt Sandra explains. "Why don't you say hello to Mirasol?"

So I rush to Mirasol's room. The door's open, but I knock anyway.

"Prima!" she says when she sees me.

"Prima!" I say back.

She waves me in and pulls out the chair from her vanity. "Sit here."

She's got long fingernails. They're painted purple to match the quinceañera dresses, and the pinkies are painted silver. She should be a hand model for bracelets and rings.

I take a seat, and right away, Mirasol starts fixing my hair. She doesn't even ask. She grabs a comb and tries pulling it through.

"You'll never get rid of all the tangles," I say, "because of the curls."

"Don't be silly," she says. "Come on." I follow her to a bathroom that's between her and Paloma's bedrooms. They call it a Jack-and-Jill bath, which makes me laugh because every time I hear those names, I think of the nursery rhyme.

Mirasol takes me to the sink and washes my hair with shampoo and conditioner for a "smooth, sleek look." After the blow dryer, she uses the flat iron to get rid of my curls, but when she's finished, my hair's still wild and curly. Instead of getting mad, she laughs. She says,

"Next time, I'll try a silicon-based straightening serum. You can't use water or mousse on your hair because any kind of moisture will cause it to frizz again."

"You know a lot about hair products," I say. "Are you going to be a stylist when you grow up?"

"No. I'm going to be the person who tests your blood when you go to the doctor. I shadowed your dad during career day and looked at blood through a microscope. It was awesome"

My dad's job is fixing medical equipment, so he's always visiting hospitals and labs. Mom has a job, too, but only part-time. She works in the gift shop at Spohn Hospital and Aunt Sandra babysits Alex while she's gone.

"Styling hair is just a hobby," Mirasol explains as she divides my hair into three sections for a braid. "Next time, we'll try a detangler, too. That's a special shampoo that's supposed to get rid of tangles."

It probably won't work, but I don't care. Having tangles is okay. It's the streak of white that bothers me.

"My hair only likes three styles," I say, "braids, ponytails, and hats."

Mirasol looks at me through the mirror and smiles. "You are so cute no matter what style of hair you have."

"I don't feel cute," I say. "I hate my birthmark. Why did my mom have to look at the lunar eclipse when she was pregnant? Why couldn't she have been watching TV instead?"

"I *like* your white hair," Mirasol says. "It's a defining feature. In fact, some people get streaks of colored hair on purpose." She gives examples of people with streaks of pink, green, or purple. All of them are famous, which means they *want* to be singled out. When I ask for people with *white* streaks, she names a few superheroes and villains. I complain that they're fictional, so she says, "How about Bonnie Raitt?"

"That's true," I say, but I don't know who Bonnie Raitt is. I agree because I don't want to sound dumb.

I wish Mirasol could name another prima or someone who lives in the neighborhood or goes to my school—an ordinary person in Corpus Christi, living an ordinary life with poliosis. I wish she could name someone with a little brother, an abuela who lives across the street, and a love for hats and rabbits. I wish she could name someone who is just like me because sometimes I can't help feeling like the only person in the world who's different.

La guitarra

Paloma returns from mariachi practice a few minutes later. She steps into Mirasol's room, guitar in hand, and bursts into "Ay, Jalisco," a famous mariachi song.

I can only understand a few of the words: "grito" (shout), "lindo" (pretty), and "palabra" (word). The rest is a blur. The music gets the attention of Alex and Little Joe. They run in and start hopping around to dance. I grab their hands, and we run in little circles while Paloma strums her guitarra and sings about "shouting pretty words." We're laughing. Even Paloma manages to chuckle between verses. Mirasol doesn't laugh, but she's clapping to the beat with a smile.

Then I let Alex and Little Joe go. They're dizzy from all the turns, so they lose their balance and bump into Mirasol's vanity, knocking over hair spray and perfume.

"Okay, that's enough," she says. "Everybody out."

She starts shooing us to the door. Alex and Little Joe run out first, but Paloma hangs back.

"Out!" Mirasol says again, this time pointing at the door. A few seconds ago, she was acting like my fairy godmother and personal stylist, but as soon as her sister appears, she changes. Why can't she be nice *all* the time?

As we are walking out, Mirasol speed-dials one of our primas and says, "You'll never believe what just happened. Little Joe and Alex tackled my vanity and broke my favorite bottle of perfume."

Paloma shakes her head as we continue down the hallway.

"What a liar, right?" I say.

"You know it," Paloma says, laughing. Then she grabs my braid and gives it a playful tug. "Look at your locks. You are so cute, Luna. That's why you're one of my favorite cousins."

"Really? You like me better than Claudia?"

She thinks about it. "Claudia can be cool sometimes, but I don't talk to her very much. She likes to tell on me, and she can't keep any secrets."

It's true. I can't say or do anything without Claudia

reporting to the teacher or my parents or *her* parents or all of my primas and friends. Apparently, Paloma can't say or do anything, either.

When we enter her room, she puts away her instrument and closes the door to the Jack-and-Jill restroom because we can hear Mirasol talking to whoever's on the other end, probably Celeste.

"So what's this about flash cards?" Paloma asks as she plops on her bed. "When I got home from rehearsal, your mom thanked me for helping you make them. I had no idea what she was talking about, but I said 'you're welcome' anyway."

I tell her about my Spanish grade, how I got an F on a test and a C on my last assignment.

"Why isn't Claudia helping?" Paloma asks. "Isn't she in your class?"

"Yes," I admit. "But you know how competitive she is. She'll probably tell me 'silla' means 'carpet' when I know that it really means 'chair,' and she'll lie just so she could get higher grades."

Paloma shakes her head. "Primas are supposed to help each other, not mess each other up." She reaches for a pad of Post-its on the bedside table. "I don't have any flash cards," she says, "but I can make you a list of Spanish words."

"That would be great!" I say.

She takes a Post-it, writes "la cama," and sticks it on her bed. Then she writes "el espejo" and puts it on the mirror. She does the same for door (la puerta), lamp (la lámpara), and book (el libro). I already know how to say "book" and "door" in Spanish, but the other words are new. Soon, Paloma's got Post-its on a dozen items, and she points at them, making me repeat and memorize. After reviewing a few times, she takes away the Post-its and quizzes me. I miss two, so we do it again. This time, I get all of them right.

"See?" she says, delighted. "You're going to get a perfect score on your next Spanish test. I just know it!"

"I guess so," I say.

"What's wrong? You don't seem convinced."

How do I explain? Knowing words is fine, but even if I learned a hundred words in Spanish, I still wouldn't know how to put them together.

"I need to learn sentences," I tell Paloma. "When we do Spanish skits, we have to say full sentences."

"Okay," she says. "Repeat after me."

I nod and straighten up so I can concentrate. I can't wait to learn more, but instead of giving me everyday sentences, Paloma gives me lyrics to her mariachi songs. She's not singing, but I can recognize the words. Plus, I have no idea what I'm saying. How can I say a Spanish sentence without knowing what it means?

"Wait," I say. "This isn't working. The mariachi songs are not going to help me write skits."

She sighs. "Hmmm . . . It's hard to come up with sentences when I don't know what you want to talk about."

"I just want to be able to respond to things in Spanish. Like, how do I say 'yes' and 'no way' or 'that's cool' or 'how's it going?' Normal stuff like that."

She nods. "Okay. So you just want to shoot the breeze."

"Yeah! That's it."

Now that she understands, Paloma jumps right into her lesson. "Say '¡Chale!' for 'Give me a break!' or 'No way!' Say '¡Dale shine!' for 'Hurry up!' 'Juega la fría' means 'play it cool' and 'vato barrato' means 'lazy dude.' When you're greeting someone, you can say '¿Cómo te va todo?' and when you're leaving, you can say 'Hasta luego.' And one of my favorite things to say is '¡A la chambirdies!'" It sounds like "ham birdies," not like a Spanish word at all.

"What does 'a la chambirdies' mean?"

She shrugs. "I made it up. It doesn't really have a meaning, but when it's time to say it, you'll feel it in your bones—like when you say 'Whoa!' or 'Woo-hoo!' or 'Yikes!' I mean, what do those words mean, right?" I nod. "Yet when it's time," she goes on, "they just come out of your mouth on their own."

It makes total sense to me, and I couldn't be happier. Finally, I'm learning Spanish that I can use!

"Primas!" we hear, and when we turn around, there's Kimberly walking into the bedroom. She's in sixth grade, middle school like Paloma, but they aren't at the same school. Kimberly's always building something, so I can't wait to ask about her latest project. Last year, she made a lot of birdhouses.

Before I can say anything, Kimberly holds up her thumb. It's wrapped in a bandage. "I accidentally hit it with a hammer when I was helping my dad build a fence," she explains.

"Ouch," Paloma says, and then, "Are Uncle Freddy and Tía Nena here, too?"

I startle. "They're coming?" I don't mean to sound freaked out, but they're Claudia's parents. She's the last person I want to see today.

"No," Kimberly says. "They aren't coming after all."

"Why not?" Paloma asks. "The reason we're having a fish fry is because Uncle Freddy and my dad went fishing on the new boat."

"It's not new," I say. "It's previously owned and the seats are cracked." I expect them to laugh, but they don't. They just keep talking.

"I heard that Tía Nena is allergic to seafood," Kimberly says.

"No way!" Paloma laughs. "Uncle Freddy bought a boat and his wife can't even eat what he catches?"

"That's so funny," I say, but no one pays attention. They don't even glance in my direction.

"As soon as Tía Nena touches, smells, or eats seafood," Kimberly explains, "her hands swell up and her fingers get purple because her rings cut off her circulation."

"Ow! That must hurt," I say, but again, they have forgotten about me. They just go on and on about Tía Nena's allergies. I'm invisible!

One minute, Mirasol is being nice to me, and the next minute, she's throwing me out of her room. Then Paloma's giving me all her attention, but as soon as Kimberly arrives, she ignores me. I know it's because I'm younger, but age shouldn't matter. I'm only a couple of years behind. It shouldn't make a difference.

That's *another* reason friends are better than cousins. A friend listens to you *all* the time, not only when it's convenient or when no one else is around.

Soon, we hear our parents calling for dinner. We head to the kitchen, and my prima Josie is there helping out. She's Kimberly's sister and taller than everyone, even my uncles. Because she's so tall, she had to be the last dama during the procession at Mirasol's quinceañera. She stoops as she walks, but she still stands out. She hates being tall as much as I hate having a streak of white hair. I guess everybody has something to be embarrassed about.

The kitchen island has Mom's coleslaw and watermelon. There are also hush puppies, french fries, and the golden fillets of fish that my uncles caught after they went fishing in the new, but really used, boat and discovered that if Tía Nena eats seafood, her hands will swell, her hair will fall out, and her skin will get red splotches. Poor Tía Nena!

Wait a minute! *Her* bad luck is really *my* good luck because I don't have to see Claudia today. *Woo-hoo!* I think.

We serve ourselves and squeeze around the table, our elbows bumping as we eat. The fish has tiny bones, but it's delicious. When we're done, Abuela takes out the banana pudding, and we stuff our faces again. Then we all sit around, half-asleep from so much food.

When Uncle Joe starts to snore, Aunt Sandra slaps his shoulder.

"Hey, vato barrato," she says, "help me clean up."

I glance at Paloma when I hear "vato barrato." She winks back.

"¡A la chambirdies!" I say.

Everyone gives me a puzzled look and Paloma shakes her head as if to say "not now." I guess I still don't understand what it means, but if I say it for different situations, I'll eventually get it right. Then I'll be bilingual just like everybody else.

Otra vez

It's Monday, time for school again. There's Claudia, sitting in my chair and eating my breakfast again, this time a pumpkin empanada from the bag of pan dulce my dad bought. Without looking, I know it's the last empanada because that's my favorite, and Claudia likes to eat the last of everything. Sure enough, I peek in the bag and all that's left are two conchas, puffy breads with pink or white powdered sugar. They're called conchas because they look like shells. I grab one, take a bite, and chew. It tastes okay, but I'd rather have the empanada.

Claudia's backpack is hanging from the chair. She reaches into it and pulls out a skein of yarn. "I bought green since it's your favorite color."

"Oh," I say. "That's nice." But it's *not* nice because she bought the wrong kind of green. Instead of green like cute frogs or emeralds, Claudia's yarn is green like seaweed.

"On Mondays, we meet for Needle Beetles," she says. "I'm going to learn how to knit, and next month, kickball starts. I can't wait."

"It's nice to see you getting so involved," Mom tells my prima. Then she turns to me. "And you, Lucky Luna? You haven't mentioned any clubs this year."

I shrug because I haven't joined anything yet. Last year, I was in Newsletter with Mabel, but it felt like another writing class. Then I joined Pet Pals, thinking I could take care of a rabbit and show my parents how responsible I am. But we don't have any rabbits at our school. We have fish, lizards, snakes, turtles, and hamsters, and the only thing Pet Pals did was clean their tanks and cages once a week.

"Well?" Mom asks.

"I'm still figuring it out," I say. "Maybe there's a club for hats or a cooking class."

She smiles. "A cooking class sounds like fun. Let me know what you need." She's acting like I already signed up, but I just said the first thing that came to mind. Then again, if I take a cooking class, I can learn how to make empanadas and blueberry muffins and pancakes so I can have the breakfast I want instead of the leftovers Claudia leaves behind.

Then it's time for school. I remember my hair and sigh about not having a hat. Three weeks to go. That's almost as long as the entire life span of a mosquito or fly—which means . . . if I were a mosquito or fly, I'd have to go my entire life without hats!

Stop obsessing, I tell myself, so on the way to the bus, I ask Claudia about her mom's allergies. "Is it true that the last time she ate fish, her throat closed up and you had to call the ambulance so they could save her life?"

"No," she says. "Where did you get that idea?"

"Paloma told me. Or maybe it was Mirasol or Kimberly. I can't remember."

"Oh? When did you talk to *them*?"

"Saturday. At the fish fry."

"You went?"

"Yes, they invited me. They *always* invite me places."

"Me too," she says. "I get invited everywhere, all the time. But the reason we didn't go to the fish fry is because my mom doesn't like seafood. She's not allergic. She just doesn't like how it tastes."

"Then why did your dad buy a boat?"

"Because he likes fishing and because there's lots of other things to do on a boat. You can go for a ride to see the city and all the mansions along Ocean Drive. You can enjoy the peace and quiet while you rock with the little waves and eat fried chicken from KFC."

"You mean the fried chicken your mom threw at the boat along with the mashed potatoes and coleslaw?"

"She didn't—" Claudia shakes her head. "Oh, never

mind. If I say something, you'll just make it bigger than it really is."

"No, I won't."

"Yes, you will."

"I won't!" I can't believe she thinks I'd exaggerate or lie.

Just then, we spot the bus down the street and run to the corner. Luckily, we don't miss it, but it's *unlucky*, too, because now I have to go to school, hatless, when I'd rather stay at home, where I can at least *look* at my favorite sombreros.

When we step onto the bus, a boy says, "There was an old lady who lived in a shoe." I give him the stink-eye. Then a girl pinches her nose, and *Claudia* gives *her* the stink-eye. My stink-eye and hers are enough to shut them up, but just to make sure they don't start up again, I take a few more seconds to glare. I'm not shy. I make eye contact, and if my eyes were jellyfish, they'd be stinging every bully.

I sit beside Mabel. She asks if I'm okay, and I tell her that I can't wait to wear hats again.

We ride in silence for a while. Then I say, "Did you join any clubs? Besides Newsletter, I mean."

"Not yet. Why? Want to join something together?"

"That would be great," I say. "But we can't join Needle Beetles because Claudia's already in that club."

Mabel raises her eyebrows. I can tell she doesn't like how I avoid Claudia, but she doesn't say anything about it. "Well, we can't join anything that meets on Tuesdays because that's when I have Newsletter, but any other day of the week is fine." We fist-bump, our way of shaking hands when we make a deal. "Speaking of which," she adds, "I'm in charge of the Spotlight column this year." Last year, the Spotlight column had articles about new teachers, school programs, and remodeling projects at our school. It's the only column that's interesting, so I'm glad that Mabel's in charge. "I'm going to interview Claudia during recess," Mabel says, "so I can write a profile since she just joined our school. It'll have her picture *and* a paragraph."

I can't believe she's writing about Claudia. Maybe she hasn't thought it through. "Can't you write about someone else? Claudia's not that interesting."

"I thought you'd be happy. I'm just trying to make your cousin feel welcome."

"She feels welcome," I say. I can tell she's not going to change her mind, so I make a suggestion. "Why don't I help you come up with some questions?" I hold my fist close to her mouth, pretending it's a microphone. "Hello, Claudia, when do you plan to return to Sacred Heart?'"

Mabel brushes my hand away. "She's not going back. Just accept it. Besides, I have to do the interview alone. You'll distract us."

"No, I won't. Promise."

"Luna, I've known you since first grade." That's her way of saying that no matter how much I promise, I won't be able to stop myself from getting in the way.

"Fine," I say. "But you better write a true profile. You better show Claudia the way she *really* is."

"I will because I have to be objective. That's an important part of being a good journalist."

When we get to school, Mabel and I check the club board. Some clubs last all year long, but others are only for a month. It depends on the topic. I scan the sheets—no hats, no rabbits, no cooking, no luck. There's a board game group, but it's on the same day as Mabel's Newsletter. There's Ping-Pong, but Mabel's not interested.

"What're you doing?" John-John asks, squeezing between Mabel and me.

"Looking for a club," Mabel answers. "Luna and I want to join the same thing but we're not having any luck."

"You should join *my* club," John-John tells me. "I'm in Community Gardeners. Next week, we're planting tomatoes and cabbages."

"And flowers?" I ask.

"Probably some flowers, but you can't eat those. I joined because we'll have to grow our own food when the zombie apocalypse comes."

"We'll need flowers, too," I say, "for hope."

"That's right," Mabel adds. "I just heard about a girl whose plane fell apart in the middle of the sky, and she fell to the ground, still strapped in her seat. No one else survived, not even her mother. Can you imagine wandering through the Amazon jungle with nothing to eat and only one shoe? All those bugs biting you, day and night? And without your glasses when you really need them to see? She wandered around for ten days before someone found her. And what kept her alive? Hope. I saw it on an episode of *Mysteries at the Museum*."

John-John thinks about it. "I guess we'll need hope, too. We don't want to lose the will to survive. We might just *give* ourselves to the zombies if that happens."

He makes a good point. "Gardens it is," I decide.

I find the sign-up sheet. There are a few openings left. I write my name and grab a flyer that lists the supplies. Maybe I can plant carrots, too, for when I finally get a rabbit.

Buenos días

The bell rings, so we hurry to class. "Good morning," Mr. Cruz says when we walk in.

I decide to try out my Spanish. "Buenos días, Señor Cruz. ¿Cómo te va todo?"

He smiles. "Muy bien. Muy bien." That means "very well, very well." I don't know why he says it twice.

It's another boring day in class. In language arts, we get a new spelling list with words that end in "i-b-l-e" like "gullible," "horrible," "permissible," and "invisible." I know what some, but not all, of the words mean. Believe it or not, English is sometimes a foreign language, too. Luckily, Mr. Cruz lets us use a dictionary so we can write sentences that make sense. I write:

1. Nothing is more horrible than going to school with your prima.

2. My mother is gullible because she believes the lies my prima tells about me.

3. I wish it were permissible to scream at my prima when she gets on my nerves.

4. I also wish I were invisible when people make jokes about my white streak of hair.

When we're done, Mr. Cruz invites us to share. I don't volunteer. Neither does Claudia, but after a few students read their sentences, she raises her hand.

"There's a lot of other words that end in 'i-b-l-e.' Like 'sensible,' 'incontrovertible,' and 'feasible.' We should add them to the list."

"I think we have enough words for this week," Mr. Cruz says, "but you just gave me a great idea." He turns to the whole class. "If anyone would like to earn some extra credit, see if you can find at least three other words that end in 'i-b-l-e.' Remember, don't use words that your classmates have already found. We'll keep a list on the board for everyone to see." He grabs a blue marker and writes Claudia's words, which probably means she's getting extra credit without even trying.

I look around, and I can't believe it! Claudia has just created more work, but instead of being mad, my fellow students seem happy. They *want* to find more words.

They think it's a competition. *Well, I'll show them,* I think.

I raise my hand, and Mr. Cruz calls on me. "Can I add my three words right now?" He offers the marker, so I go to the board. I write "unforgettible," "predictible," and "disposible."

I turn around and glance at Claudia. She has a smirk on her face, probably because she's jealous, but then Mr. Cruz says, "I applaud your effort, Luna, but these words are misspelled. They don't end in 'i-b-l-e.' They end in '*a*-b-l-e.'"

He starts erasing them. No wonder Claudia gave me that look. She wasn't jealous. She was gloating. She *knew* I was wrong. Now the whole world is going to know, too, including my parents, aunts, uncles, and primas.

"I didn't know how to spell those words, either," Mabel says when I sit down.

"Me neither," John-John adds.

I don't believe them. They're just trying to make me feel better when the only thing that works is drinking water. I grab my bottle and take a sip. It's nice and cool. It washes away my frustration, just like Abuela promised.

Next is science. Since it's hurricane season, we're studying the weather. Mr. Cruz shows us the website for the National Hurricane Center and hands out maps with a grid of dotted lines. There's a tropical disturbance at 23° north and 75° west. It's way over there on the other side of Florida, so I don't know why we need to care. Plus, it's a tropical *disturbance*, which is not as bad as a tropical *storm*, which is not as bad as a hurricane.

Mr. Cruz explains how hurricanes form. He's got a slideshow with diagrams, and he's using a lot of words about weather. When he gets to "atmospheric pressure," Claudia raises her hand again. "Last year at Sacred Heart," she says, "we learned to make a barometer using plastic wrap, a can, and a straw."

"That sounds like an interesting project," Mr. Cruz says. Then, to the class, "Would anyone else like to learn how to make a barometer?"

"For extra credit?" someone asks.

Mr. Cruz agrees to the extra credit, and about ten hands go up, including John-John's! Mabel *almost* raises her hand, but then she stops herself because if *I'm* not going to make a barometer, *she* isn't, either.

Claudia just created another assignment, but instead of rolling their eyes, the students thank her. It seems like they've even forgotten about her giant nose. What is wrong with them? Am I in a parallel universe? That happens on *Star Trek* sometimes.

Otra vez, I grab my water bottle. I nearly drink the whole thing.

Later we head out for recess, and I tug Mr. Cruz's sleeve. "Can I run to the restroom?" I ask. "It's an emergency."

"You've been going to the restroom a lot lately. Are you sick? Is everything okay?"

"Yes," I say. "I just have to go."

He has a worried look on his face but nods anyway, so I run down that hall as fast as I can.

When I finally get outside for recess, Mabel and Claudia are sitting on a bench. Mabel has a notebook, and she's writing notes. I know she wants to be a journalist when she grows up, but that doesn't mean she should interview Claudia. Journalists interview famous people, so she should focus on the famous people of our school like the principal, the smartest student in each grade, and anybody who wins an award. Claudia's only been here a week. She hasn't won anything yet and probably never will.

I search for John-John and find him on the basketball court. It has six hoops, and groups of kids are trying to make baskets. He's with Josh, Tamara, and Luke.

"Can I join?"

Instead of answering, Luke throws me the ball, and I try a layup. It hits the bottom edge of the backboard. We take turns. Tamara makes a free throw, no problem. Josh's ball circles the rim, keeping us in suspense but falling out at the last moment. Luke tries a three-pointer and misses, but John-John gets the rebound and scores. Then it's my turn again. I shoot, granny-style, and the ball flies over the backboard, rolling on the grass beyond.

"I'm better at volleyball," I explain.

Then recess is over and we head back to class. When Mr. Cruz says it's time for math, I say, "¡Chale!" A few kids giggle, but *he* doesn't look pleased at all.

When he hands out a worksheet and takes forever to get to my row, I say, "Dale shine." He raises an eyebrow, questioning me, so I use the other word for "hurry." "¡Ándale!" His eyebrow stays up, and I wonder if he knows what "dale shine" and "ándale" mean.

When he catches Ryan doodling instead of doing his work, I say, "Hey, Ryan, quit being a vato barrato." A bunch of kids laugh, but Mr. Cruz gets a stern look on his face. Before he can scold us, I say, "Juega la fría, my friends." But they don't play it cool. They laugh even louder.

Mr. Cruz says, "Luna, maybe you can work quietly now."

He hasn't raised his voice, but I can tell he's mad. Claudia's shaking her head, which means she's going to tell my mom for sure. I'm trying my best to be good— I'm even speaking Spanish when I don't have to!—but for some reason, I'm still in all kinds of trouble.

El problema

One of the easiest Spanish words to learn is "problema." It means problem. Basically, it's an English word with an "a" stuck at the end. In Texas, lots of people stick an "o" at the end instead because they like to say "no problemo." I wish we could do that with *all* Spanish words. Then "desk" would be "desk-o" and a Snickers bar would be "Snickers-o" and "Give me a break" would be "Dame un break-o." I should be glad that *some* Spanish words sound like English because there are languages—Japanese, Greek, and Tagalog—that don't sound close to English at all.

The reason I'm thinking about having a problema is because as soon as I get home, Mom asks me to sit down. Then she takes a seat beside me and says, "I heard you had an interesting day."

Sometimes "interesting" means "fascinating," but

other times, it means "weird." So I'm trying to figure out if my day was fascinating or weird, but as far as I can tell, it was just a regular day. So why would Mom ask about a regular day? And why would she ask me to sit as if she's about to share terrible news and is worried I'll faint from the shock? And what does she mean by "I heard"?

"Heard? From who?" I ask. Then I figure it out. "Did Claudia squeal again? When did she have time? I thought she had Needle Beetles after school."

"I haven't talked to Claudia," Mom explains. "Mr. Cruz called a few minutes ago."

When teachers call, it's for bad news, never for good. Trust me. Teachers have called my house many times, and they have never shared good news.

"Did Mr. Cruz tell you that I misspelled three words? Because they weren't on the official spelling list. They were for extra credit, so even if I misspelled them, it's no big deal."

"No, we didn't talk about spelling."

"Did he call because I grabbed my red and black crayons and turned my hurricane map into a chessboard? I don't know why it matters. I can still plot the storms if I use markers."

"We didn't—"

"Was it because I complained about math and told him to hurry up with the worksheets and called Ryan a lazy dude and then told the whole class to play it cool because they were laughing and Mr. Cruz seemed a little annoyed? If you think about it, I was just trying to help him keep the class focused."

"Luna Ramos!" Mom says. Adding my last name is her way of telling me to be quiet. "He called because you keep asking for the restroom pass. He's worried you're sick because each time you ask, it seems . . . well . . . urgent. He says you're going almost every hour." She touches my forehead. "Are you feeling sick, mija?"

I brush her hand away. "No, I'm fine. I'm just drinking a lot of water. *A lot* of water. It's because of Abuela's wise advice. She told me to drink water when I feel stressed, and I've been really, really stressed because Claudia's in my class, spying all the time and coming up with homework ideas, and because I can't wear hats."

Mom studies me a moment. "Well, maybe you should try a different strategy. Drinking water is good, but you shouldn't be going to the bathroom every hour."

I think about it and come up with a great idea. "I could wear hats again," I suggest. "And Claudia could move to another fifth-grade class."

Mom sighs. "In the real world . . ."

And that's when I tune Mom out, because every time she begins a sentence with "in the real world," something bad follows. When I asked if we could go to Antarctica to see penguins in their natural environment, she told me that in the real world, money doesn't grow on trees. When she caught me trying to catch a frog so I could kiss him, she told me that in the real world, frogs don't turn into princes. And when she heard me chanting rhyming spells that were supposed to turn my mean, annoying primas into mosquitoes, she told me that in the real world, magic doesn't exist and that's why you can't kiss frogs or wish upon stars or tap your red shoes three times. I was in third grade. I knew there wasn't magic but I *hoped*. "Aren't superstitions like magic?" I asked. "And don't you believe in *them*?" Instead of replying, she crossed her arms and somehow made her line of consternation deeper than it was when the conversation started.

I wish the real world *did* have magic. Sure, I might use it to turn my primas into mosquitoes when I get mad, but I'd do nice things, too—like turn all carrots into carrot cake and all bananas into banana bread. Think of how sweet the world could be.

"Luna?" I hear Mom say. "Lucky Luna, are you listening?"

"Um . . . kinda?"

"I was saying that you can't always get what you want, so you have to learn to accept your situation even when you don't like it. Sometimes you have to work with people you don't like. It might not be a prima. It might be someone at your job, and if you don't learn to get along, you might lose that job. You won't be able to wear hats all the time, either. Some jobs require uniforms, and most uniforms don't have hats. If you don't follow the dress code, you'll lose that job, too. Do you understand?"

"Yes," I say, defeated. "I'll never be able to keep a job because everything I do will get me fired."

Mom chuckles. "You'll be fine as long as you accept that Claudia's not going anywhere and that you're still grounded from wearing hats." Then she gets a serious look on her face. "To be honest, one of the reasons I took them away is because I want you to accept yourself—*all* of yourself, even your hair."

"I do, but the other kids . . ." I pause, hating to remember the jokes they've been making. "Their comments are another reason I keep drinking water and rushing to the restroom every five minutes."

"Give them a chance," Mom says. "They'll change. In the meantime, you need another way to deal with feeling stressed." She heads to the kitchen, and I follow. Once there, she reaches into a high cabinet for a giant shoebox. She removes the lid. "These are stress balls. Pick one."

I peek and find squishy shapes inside. Some are round balls with logos for places like Ace Hardware or Roger's Pharmacy. But there are other shapes, too. There's a polar bear, soda can, fire hydrant, and pig. I search for a rabbit but no luck. So I pick a purple starfish instead. It says "Mustang Island" on its underside.

"Next time you're feeling stressed," Mom explains. "Squeeze the starfish."

"That's it?" I ask. When she nods, I say, "Can I still drink water?"

"Of course. But not so much. Now go do your homework before it gets too late."

So I go to my room and take out my books, but I don't do homework right away. I stare at my starfish. Last year at the Texas State Aquarium, I learned some interesting things—like starfish are not fish at all. They're actually related to the sand dollar, which I thought was a seashell, not an animal. Starfish also regrow arms that get chopped off, and they have spines for protection. I run my hand over the spongy starfish. It doesn't have spines, and I don't have hats. In a way, we're the same because there's nothing to protect us from the mean kids in this world.

El nombre

I already mentioned that lots of my primas are named after things that hang in the sky, but I also have a fourth-grade cousin whose name is Marina, which is related to the sea because that's where you park boats. She has pictures where she stands beside the signs—Corpus Christi Municipal Marina, Cove Harbor Marina, Bluffs Landing Marina, and Fulton Beach Marina. So when she calls me on Skype, instead of "hello," I say, "Marina, want to go to the marina?"

She says, "Yes!" even though we can't go because it's a school night. "But that isn't why I called," she goes on. "I just finished Skyping with Claudia, and she told me a funny story. She said you were using lots of slang—in Spanish!"

"No, I wasn't."

"But you said 'vamos a lunchar' and 'dale shine' and 'juega la fría' and 'ya te watcheo, güey.'"

I hear her poodle yapping in the background. It sounds like he's agreeing with her, like he's saying "Yup! Yup! Yup!" Marina has lots of pets and all of them are named after streets in Corpus Christi. Her poodle's called Weber.

"I didn't say *all* those things," I explain, "but yeah, I said *some* of them."

"But that isn't real Spanish," Marina says. "It's like pointing at your friends and saying, 'Here's my squad,' or getting mad at someone and saying, 'I'm going to throw some shade on that girl.'"

Here's my squad? Throw some shade? I have no idea what she's talking about.

Before I can ask what she means, she goes on. "And Claudia said the other kids thought you were being funny, so they laughed, which just made you show off more."

"I wasn't—"

"Then the teacher forbid you from saying another word, so you had to do sign language the rest of the day and no one knew what you were talking about but that was okay because Claudia said that no one *ever* knows what you're talking about."

I don't answer. I just squint my eyes real hard, pretending I could shoot electricity and make it run through cyberspace to zap Claudia for telling lies about me and Marina for believing them, and . . .

"Paloma!" I say. "This is all her fault! I thought she was helping, but she was tricking me the whole time!"

"*Paloma* told you to say those things?"

"She was giving me Spanish lessons, but instead of teaching me real words, she must have taught me fake ones."

Marina gets serious. "So now you're mad at Paloma and you're going to find a way to get revenge?"

"Yes . . . no . . . that's not what I said. I mean I'm mad but—"

"Don't worry," Marina says. "I'm on your side. A prima should never cause another prima to get embarrassed. I'm sure Celeste and Estrella will take your side, too, once I tell them what happened."

"What? Don't tell any—"

But it's too late. Marina doesn't hear because she hangs up in the middle of my sentence. So now Paloma's going to think I'm mad, which I am, but I'm not going to do anything about it, except maybe go to her next mariachi performance and boo. I'm sure I can boo, smile, and clap at the same time, so when she glances over, she'll think I'm praising her, not getting revenge.

It's a good plan, but it doesn't help the way I feel right now. Right now, I'm feeling humiliated. My classmates were laughing at me because I made a fool out of myself. How can I ever face those kids again?

I need advice, so I sprint through the house. "Going to Abuela's," I tell Dad as I whir past, and less than a minute later, I'm there. "Abuela!" I call through the screen door.

"¡Pasa! ¡Pasa!" she says, waving me in.

She takes a seat on the couch and points at the rocking chair. I sit down, but then I stand up. I sit down again, and stand up again. Sit, stand, sit, stand—nothing feels comfortable because being upset on the inside makes you upset on the outside, too.

"Siéntate, por favor," Abuela says. I can tell by her hand gestures that she wants me to settle down. I sit in the rocking chair and force myself to stay there. "¿Qué pasó?" she asks.

"My primas," I say. "They're always getting me in trouble and they make fun of me because I can't really speak Spanish, but I'm not the only one. Kimberly and Josie don't speak Spanish, either, because their dad's not Mexican. No one gives *them* a hard time, but everyone gives *me* a hard time. Then, instead of teaching me, my primas make things worse. I asked Paloma for help but she just taught me slang!"

Without realizing, I've stood up again, but instead of sitting and standing, I'm pacing. Gato's watching from the coffee table, his head turning back and forth like there's an invisible string swinging before him.

"Aren't we supposed to help each other?" I say. "When Claudia came to my school last week, I introduced her to everyone and gave her a tour. I helped her catch up with the lessons. I even carried her books a few times and gave kids the stink-eye when they made fun of her nose. I was *real* nice. And I did *not* tell all my primas every single thing she did. That's being nosy, and I am *not* a nosy person. Now that I think of it, this isn't Paloma's fault at all. It's Claudia's. *She's* the one who gave Mr. Cruz the idea that a cousin could help me learn Spanish, and *she's* the one who called Marina to gossip, which made Marina call me. Now Marina's going to call my other primas to tell them I'm mad at Paloma when the person I'm *really* mad at is Claudia for starting all the chisme in the first place. What should I do, Abuela?"

I have to take a deep breath because I'm talking so fast, but it's okay. Abuela needs time to figure out what I said. She doesn't really know English, so when I speak, she hears a lot of blah, blah, blah.

Finally, she gives me her wise advice. "En boca cerrada no entran moscas."

I take a second to translate. *Blah, mouth, blah, blah, blah, flies.* Not "flies" as in soaring through the sky but "flies" as in pesky insects.

Is she talking about the tiny mouths of flies? Or is she talking about eating flies? I have no idea until I remember how superstitious my family can be. Some superstitions cause good or bad luck, but others fix things. For example, every time Alex gets hiccups, Mom pulls a thread from her own clothes and places it on his forehead to make the hiccups go away. Sometimes it takes a while, but every single time, the hiccups eventually stop.

This must be one of those fix-it superstitions, too. *Mouth and flies*, I silently repeat as I try to figure out the solution to my problem. I want Claudia to stop talking about me, so I have to do something with flies.

"You are very wise," I tell Abuela. "¡Gracias!"

She smiles. "De nada, mija."

Las moscas

I plan to catch a lot of flies today. I also plan to have first choice when it comes to breakfast. I wake up thirty minutes early, get dressed, look longingly at my hats, and rush to the kitchen before Claudia arrives, but instead of Pop-Tarts, muffins, or pan dulces, Mom's made scrambled eggs and bacon—enough for everyone!

"You're up early," Dad says. Usually, he's gone before I get to the kitchen.

"I want to start eating before Claudia gets here because she always takes my breakfast."

Mom glances at me, but she doesn't say anything.

"Early bird gets the worm," Dad says. Then he kisses the top of my head and Alex's cheek and Mom's lips before heading out.

I have another reason for getting to the kitchen before Claudia arrives. I don't want her to see me get the flyswatter. It's beneath the kitchen sink. I open the cabinet door, grab the flyswatter, and stick it in my backpack.

"Why are you taking that?" Mom asks.

I decide to tell her a half-truth, so I won't be a bold-faced liar. Besides, a half-truth has to be half-good, right? And the half-bad part goes away if you're lying to solve un problema, which is exactly what's happening here.

"We're eating snacks during recess." Before she can ask another question, I say, "Where are the envelopes?"

She walks to a drawer and hands me one. "Are you planning to write to the editor?" she teases. "Or the mayor?"

"No, but if I were, I'd tell them about the potholes. We've got a lot of potholes on our streets."

"Ain't that the truth."

I put the envelope and flyswatter in my backpack, zip it up, and serve myself a plate. Then Claudia comes in (she doesn't even knock!), grabs a plate, and serves herself eggs and bacon without asking my mom if it's okay. She's acting like this is her house, like she *belongs* here.

Soon it's time to go. I grab my water bottle, but before I can fill it, Mom takes it away. "Where's the starfish?" she asks. I pull it from my pocket, and she nods, approving. "Don't forget to squeeze it if you get stressed."

"Mom," I say through clenched lips. I don't want my

prima to hear about the starfish. Who knows what kind of stories she'll make up?

Luckily, she doesn't mention it. When we get to the bus stop, she says, "Want to see what I'm making in Needle Beetles?"

Before I can say no, she reaches into her backpack and pulls out a green ball of yarn with a shape that's not a hexagon, octagon, dodecahedron, or anything on our bulletin board. It's not even a square. I think it wants to be a circle if circles were shaped like splats of pancake mix from someone who doesn't know how to make a perfectly round pancake.

"I'm using the green yarn," she says.

I glance at it again. "That's nice." But it *isn't* nice because she bought the wrong kind of green. Instead of green like four-leaf clovers, this green is like the stuff that comes out of a caterpillar when you step on it.

"I'm making a surprise," Claudia adds. Usually, when a prima tells me something's a surprise, I beg for hints, but I don't want to seem too interested because she'll start bragging about how good she knits.

Soon the bus arrives, and when we get on, a few kids say it stinks. They're mumbling under their breath, but I can still hear them. Claudia can, too. She plops onto her seat, but instead of hiding behind a book, she starts knitting.

As soon as I sit, Mabel closes a notebook as if to hide it from me.

"What were you writing?" I ask.

"I was working on the article about your cousin."

"Really? Let me see." I reach for her notebook, but she stuffs it in her backpack before I can take a look.

"You'll have to wait for the newsletter on Friday."

"But—"

"No 'buts,'" Mabel says. "I'm not supposed to leak the story before its official publication."

"I won't talk about it," I say. "Promise."

She sighs. "Luna, I've known you since first grade."

That sentence is always like the period at the end of a conversation. Nothing I say will change her mind. I can't stand being in the dark about the article, so I reach into my pocket, grab the starfish, and squeeze. It helps, but not as much as drinking water.

We spend a couple of hours in class, and right before recess, I ask John-John and Mabel if they can help me catch flies. Mabel seems a little disgusted, but John-John's smile is wider than the Harbor Bridge. It figures. He ate an earthworm, so he must like catching flies, too. He grabs a juice box and says, "Fly bait."

"We have to keep it a secret from Claudia," I say.

Mabel crosses her arms. "What are you up to?" She sounds like my mom, and it gives me the shivers.

"It's a Mexican tradition to stop gossip," I explain. "My abuela told me about it. I'm going to put the flies in this envelope." I show it to her.

"And then?" she asks.

"Who cares?" John-John says, stuffing my fly-swatter and envelope into his camouflage backpack. "It'll be fun."

Mabel sighs but she joins us outside anyway. Turns out, I don't have to hide from Claudia because for once she's not spying on me. She's on a bench, and she's not alone. She's knitting with two other Needle Beetles. They're fifth graders from another class, so they probably haven't learned that she likes to show off and tattle.

Mabel and I follow John-John to a picnic area on the other side of the playground. He reaches into his pocket and pulls out the purple rabbit's foot. After we touch it for good luck, he says, "First we set the trap." He pours a few drops of juice on the table. "Then we wait." He takes out the flyswatter. "You need superior reflexes to catch living flies." He demonstrates, slapping the table with lightning speed. Then he hands me the flyswatter. "You try it now."

I do a few slaps as quickly as I can. "Good job," John-John says.

Then we wait for the flies to come . . . and we keep waiting . . . and the juice dries up, so we pour a little more. We wait again. Basketballs bounce on the court and hit the backboards. Jump ropes slap the pavement. Swings creak as kids go higher and higher. Our classmates are shouting, singing, and laughing. Meanwhile . . . no flies. I'm starting to feel impatient, so I squeeze the starfish. Mabel sits on the edge of the picnic table. She isn't looking at the spot of juice anymore. She's staring at the other kids having fun. I can tell she'd rather be with them, but she's loyal even if it means being completely, totally, 100 percent bored.

"We're running out of time!" I say.

John-John nods. "Agreed." He drinks the rest of his juice box and gets a new idea. "If the flies won't come to us, *we* will go to the flies."

"And where are we going to find a bunch of flies?" I ask.

He glances around. "I don't see any roadkill, so we'll have to search the Dumpsters behind the cafeteria."

"Are you kidding?" Mabel says. "That's outside the playground area."

It's against the rules to leave the playground, but . . . "I really need these flies," I say. "Besides, we'll be back before anybody notices." Mabel's not budging. "Please," I beg. "You're my best friend, and best friends are supposed to help each other, no matter what."

She thinks about it. "Okay, okay. I'm going but not to

help you get flies. I'm going to help you stay out of trouble. That means you have to listen to me, okay?"

"Okay. I promise."

We fist-bump to seal the deal. Then Mabel, John-John, and I head to the Dumpsters. When we get to the edge of the playground, we glance back to see if someone's watching. Luckily, no one's paying attention, so we run like crazy, skidding past corners, leaping over shrubs and mud scrapers, and stooping below windows so we won't get caught. Finally, we get to the back of the cafeteria and take a moment to catch our breaths. Then we spot two brown Dumpsters and catch a whiff of rotten meat and spoiled veggies. I want to gag, but I squeeze my starfish instead.

"Okay," John-John says. "Mabel, you be the lookout while Luna and I go hunting."

She nods and peeks around the edge of the building. Meanwhile, John-John and I approach the Dumpsters. He was right. There are hundreds of flies buzzing about. It's like Disneyland, but instead of excited people, we have excited bugs.

John-John flips open the giant lid. "Go for it," he says, and I get to work. I don't even have to aim because there are just so many—not only flies but roaches, bees, and ants, too. I slap the lip of the Dumpster. I slap the front wall, the side wall, even the ground. Slap! Slap! Slap!

John-John has the envelope and collects the little bodies. A few times, we scrape clean the flyswatter, getting rid of the flies that are too squished up.

"Hurry! Mrs. Carmona's coming," Mabel says. She sounds nervous because we're about to get caught.

We run off, Mabel leading us away from Mrs. Carmona's path. Once again, we skid, leap, and stoop. When we return to the playground, we're out of breath again. No one's telling jokes or being tickled, but that doesn't stop us from laughing.

Finally, we settle down. "How many did you get?" John-John asks.

We peek inside the envelope. There are about fifteen flies.

I give them a thumbs-up. "Mission accomplished."

We cheer, and Mabel says, "That was so stressful. It felt like we were in a movie. Like an action-thriller film!"

"Yeah," I say, "with mutant flies."

"And zombies!" John-John adds.

La galleta

An hour later, Claudia's behind me in the lunch line, and when I select a cookie for dessert, she tells me I should put it back and choose a fruit cup instead. "Fruit is more nutritious. Cookies have too much sugar, and too much sugar in your system can lead to diabetes and cavities. You wouldn't want a root canal, would you?"

Instead of responding, I take a giant bite of la galleta right in front of her. Claudia shakes her head and rolls her eyes. Then we pay, and instead of tagging along to my table like she did last week, she heads in another direction.

"Where are you going?" I ask.

"I'm going sit with my new friends."

"So you're not going to sit at my table anymore?"

"I thought you didn't *want* me to sit there."

"I don't but—" I can't finish the sentence. If I do, she'll know about the flies.

"But what?" she asks.

"Nothing," I say.

She does a quick turnaround. Her new friends seem happy to see her, and I have to blink a few times to make sure I'm seeing right. How'd she make friends so fast? Meanwhile, Mabel calls me to our table. I join her. Everyone's talking about an upcoming talent show, but I'm not paying attention. The envelope of moscas is in my pocket, and all I can think about is Abuela's wise advice.

"I'll be right back," I tell Mabel.

I rush to the lunch line before it closes, and while I'm waiting, I sneak a fly from my pocket. I've got some extra change, so I buy a fruit cup and drop the insect. It sinks between two grapes. Then I approach Claudia's table. She's listening to her friends, but she looks up when she sees me.

"I decided to take your advice and eat fruit," I say, holding out the cup.

"You can thank me later when your teeth don't rot."

She turns back to the conversation.

I put my fruit cup beside hers. "Look. They're exactly the same," I say. She nods without looking. *This is too easy*, I think, swapping the cups. "Well, I guess I'll go back to my table." She waves me away as if *I'm* the pesky fly.

I watch her all during lunch, and later when we're returning to class, I say, "Did you enjoy your fruit?"

Claudia shrugs. "Couldn't finish. It had a dead fly."

She doesn't say anything else. She doesn't even threaten to call the health inspector. But more important—she doesn't vow to stop gossiping! Luckily, I have more flies in the envelope.

During class, Claudia gets up to sharpen her pencil. I get up, too, dropping a fly on her desk as I walk by. She just flicks it off. Then Claudia volunteers to pick up worksheets. I leave a fly on my paper, but it slips off and lands on the floor before she sees it. When Claudia goes to the restroom, I approach Mr. Cruz's desk to ask a question, dropping a fly onto my prima's chair, but when she returns, she brushes it away before sitting. During art, I slip a fly into the water she's using to clean her brushes, but it doesn't bother her at all. She just dumps the water in the sink. Every time she sees a fly, she gets rid of it and moves on.

What's *wrong* with her? If *I* kept seeing flies, I'd wonder if it's bad luck. I'd look for cracks in the sky or holes in the earth. I'd check the Weather Channel for natural catastrophes. I would definitely stop gossiping.

Maybe she's too distracted to worry about moscas. Today some kids saw her nose and said "reek" and "stench." But she's not the only one they're talking about. I also heard "Cruella de Vil." She's a character from *101 Dalmatians*. Half her hair is black and the other half white. It hurts my feelings to hear about my hair, so it probably hurts Claudia's feelings to hear about her nose.

Finally, the dismissal bell rings. Since Mabel's staying after school to work on the newsletter, she's not riding the bus. That's a bad-luck thing. The *good*-luck thing is leaning against the window and stretching my legs because I have the whole seat to myself. It also gives me a good view of Claudia, three rows behind. She's back to knitting. Her blob-shaped circle looks bigger now.

Keeping the envelope in my lap, I take out a fly and toss it toward her, but there are boys in the rows between us. The fly hits one of them on the shoulder. I take a second fly. I don't know where it goes, but it doesn't get to Claudia. Same with the third and the fourth. I'm reaching for another when . . .

"What are you doing?" Janie says. She's standing in the aisle, her shadow falling over me. "What's in that envelope?" she wants to know.

I close the flap. "Nothing."

"Let me see," she says, and before I can stop her, she reaches across, grabs it, and peeks inside. "Gross! Are those bugs?"

"No."

"You were throwing bugs at people!"

"I was not."

But now Janie wants to make an announcement. "Hey, everybody! Luna was throwing bugs at y'all."

"That's nasty!" someone says, and someone else says, "Yeah, that stinks!" Then a bunch of kids start laughing.

"Be quiet, everyone!" Now it's Claudia talking. She isn't standing, but she looks taller. She's probably kneeling on her seat. "Leave my prima alone."

"But she was throwing bugs at you, too," Carly says.

"They're not bugs!" I shout, trying to defend myself. "They're flies!"

"Flies?" Claudia repeats.

"Same thing," Janie says. Then, to Claudia, "And Carly's right. She was throwing them at you, too. She was probably *aiming* at you."

Claudia looks at me with eyes that can peer into the darkest corners of my soul. "Well, that's between Luna and me," she says.

Just then, the bus stops. We aren't at a light or stop sign or railroad track or official stop on our route. "Settle down!" the bus driver shouts. "All of you! And no standing in the aisle!"

Janie returns to her place beside Carly. Claudia sits down and starts knitting again. And I sink as low as I can, but even with a whole seat to myself, I can't sink low enough to disappear.

Luckily, the bus reaches my stop a few minutes later. As soon as my prima and I walk into the house, Claudia marches to my mom and says, "Luna threw bugs at me.

She tried to hit me with dead flies. She even put them in my food!"

"I did not!" I throw down my backpack to show how serious I am.

"I had to go hungry," Claudia whines. "I didn't eat a single bite. And all day, I felt creepy-crawlies on my skin." She rubs her arms and shivers. "Luna even ruined my art project by throwing flies in my paint."

"That's not what happened!" I say. "I threw them in your *water*."

"See?" Claudia points at me. "She admits it. And on the bus, she *kept* throwing flies. The other kids saw it, too. The bus driver had to stop in the middle of the street because the kids were freaking out about the bugs." She turns on the dramatics. "It was humiliating! I hate flies! They're worse than roaches."

"What?" I'm beside myself. "Roaches are way worse, especially when they're in your underwear drawer. Besides, you didn't notice the flies. You flicked them away like it was no big deal."

"Well, it *was* a big deal!" she insists. "I was just trying to keep it cool in front of the other kids."

"I don't understand," Mom says to me. "Why were you throwing flies at your prima in the first place?"

"Abuela told me to. It's a Mexican tradition."

"*I've* never heard of that tradition," Claudia says. "And there's no way Abuela told you to throw flies."

"Well, you don't know everything. And she did. You can ask her yourself."

"I will!" Claudia says, and she stomps over to Abuela's, letting the door slam behind her.

Mom grabs my backpack and plops it on the table. Then she reaches in and takes out the flyswatter. For a moment, I think she's going to slap me with it, but she returns it to the space beneath the kitchen sink. Then she stares out the window. I can tell she's mad. "I don't know where to begin, Lucky Luna. Seems like every day you're fighting with Claudia, no matter the consequences. Am I supposed to keep thinking up punishments? Nothing works." She sighs heavily. "I think I'll let your dad handle this when he comes home. For now, you can go to your room and think."

So I go to my room, and when Dad comes home, he steps in, pulls out my desk chair, and sits down. He's already heard the story from Mom.

"What did Abuela say exactly?" he asks.

"She said that if I want Claudia to keep her mouth shut and stop gossiping about me, I'll have to give her flies."

"Those were her exact words?"

"No. Her exact words were in Spanish, but I can't speak Spanish, remember?"

"Then what makes you think she told you to throw flies?"

"Because she said 'boca' and 'moscas,' and I know what *those* words mean, so I filled in the blanks."

Dad thinks for a minute. "En boca cerrada no entran moscas?"

"Yes! That's it exactly. See? I was just doing what Abuela told me to do."

He leans forward, rests his elbows on his knees. "Luna, she wasn't telling you to give Claudia flies. She was telling you a dicho."

I have no idea what he's talking about. It must show on my face because he goes on to explain.

"A dicho is a Spanish proverb. She's saying that flies can't get in a closed mouth, but she doesn't mean it word for word. It's a figurative way of saying 'don't gossip.' Like when we tell you 'don't put your eggs in one basket.' You understand?"

I nod even though I once asked for a second basket during an Easter egg hunt because of that phrase. I felt so dumb when I realized it was a figure of speech. I thought I was smarter now, but apparently, Spanish and English have something in common—you can't take everything word for word.

La noche

Later that night, there's more gossip! I'm at my mirror, trying on different hats and searching for the one that matches my mood. But I'm frustrated, confused, angry, and embarrassed—too many emotions for one hat. Then I hear the Skype melody. It's Marina again.

"Prima!" she says, and I answer back with a bummed-out "Hey."

She's fast-talking. "I told Celeste and Estrella about Paloma giving you fake words and making you get in trouble at school, and they agree that it's *totally* wrong and *completely* against the prima code, so now they're mad at Paloma, too. Estrella lent her a cell phone cover, a pink one with lots of bling, and she's going to get it back. Celeste is going to break their Snapchat streak. You know how Paloma loves Snapchat. *I'm* going to unfriend her on all my social media, and I'm not going to put her back until she apologizes publicly, maybe at her next mariachi performance. I mean, really, how could she tell you that 'cama' means 'camel'? That is just plain wrong."

I'm waiting for her to take a breath so I can tell her that I'm not mad at Paloma because it's really Claudia's fault.

"I also talked to Kimberly," Marina says, "but she always takes Paloma's side. *Always*. And she told me Josie's taking her side, too. When I told her how you humiliated yourself by using fake Spanish, she said it's your fault because you didn't double-check the definitions before you went around acting like you were bilingual, and so *I* told *her* that primas aren't supposed to lie, that if you ask a prima for the color of the sky, then she better say 'blue' unless it's night or sunset time, but you know what I mean, right?"

"Right, but—"

"Don't worry. I'll make sure our primas know what's *really* going on so you can have more people on your side."

With that, she hangs up, and before I can take a breath, my computer chimes again. It's Celeste and Estrella. They're sisters, so both are on the screen at the same time.

When I answer, Celeste starts talking without bothering to say hello. "Is it true that Paloma told you 'cama' means 'casserole'?"

Then Estrella jumps in. "That's not what she said, Celeste. She told Luna that it means 'camo' like 'camouflage.'"

"Are you sure it wasn't 'casserole' or 'cantaloupe'?"

"Camo!"

"Or Camry, like the car?"

"Camo as in camouflage. Pay attention."

They go back and forth like this. I don't even know why they called if they're not going to let me talk.

Finally, I wave my arms and say, "Primas! I'm right here!"

"Don't worry," Celeste tells me. "This prima war is not your fault. You were just trying to learn something, and since Paloma's older, she thought she could take advantage of you. Well, no one takes advantage of my little prima."

"That's right," Estrella adds with a firm nod, and with that, they hang up.

I can't believe everybody's mad at everybody else. Sure, my primas get on my nerves, but the last thing I want is for us to fight. I'm ready to pull out my hair because of how stressed I feel—okay, maybe not *all* my hair but at least the white streak.

I grab the starfish instead. I squeeze and squeeze, but instead of feeling more relaxed, my arm's getting sore.

Just then, Alex walks in. He takes a few steps toward my hatcase and then glances at me because my hats are off-limits to him. Today, though, I'm too upset about other things to care. When he realizes I won't stop him, he grabs my white cowboy hat, the one I wore to Mirasol's quinceañera. He puts it on and laughs because it's too big and covers half his face.

"Here," I say, grabbing a baseball cap. It's still too big but a Velcro strap lets me adjust the size. He is too cute. "I love you," I say.

"Me too," he answers.

"You love yourself?"

"Me love *you*," he says.

He gives me a big hug, and then he runs off, still wearing my cap.

That's it. A little love from my brother makes me realize what I have to do—spread love instead of gossip. I go back to my computer and Skype Paloma. She doesn't answer. I call a second time. She still doesn't answer. I try a third time, and Mirasol picks up.

"She doesn't want to talk to you," Mirasol says. Paloma's standing behind her, glaring. "You've got half our primas yelling at her for something she didn't do."

"I did *not* tell you that 'cama' means 'llama'!" Paloma shouts over her sister's shoulder.

"I know," I say. "I don't even know where all those weird definitions came from." Then I tell her the whole story. How I used the phrases she taught me in class and how Claudia told Marina that I made a fool out of myself and how Marina turned it into this giant fight when I don't want to fight at all.

She's still behind Mirasol. "You really didn't say I taught you fake words?"

"Not exactly."

She crosses her arms and glares again.

"I was mad for about five minutes when I found out you taught me slang, because if I wrote those phrases on a test, I would probably get an F."

"But you said you wanted to learn everyday words. I was just showing you how people talk when they're *not* taking tests, like in *real* conversations."

"She's got a point," Mirasol says. She isn't looking in the camera. She's flipping through a magazine. She's not really interested in what we're saying, but she stays there like a guard dog.

"I know," I say to Paloma. "That's why I'm not mad at you. I'm really mad at Claudia, but that doesn't matter anymore. I'm sorry about this whole mess, even though I didn't start it and even though I didn't call a bunch of primas and tell them to take sides. Do you forgive me?"

She sighs, but then she uncrosses her arms and leans over Mirasol's shoulder. "I forgive you."

"Great. Are you friends now?" Mirasol asks. "Because I'm tired of babysitting."

"You aren't babysitting," Paloma says.

Mirasol grabs her magazine and stands up. "Well, that's what it feels like." She blows me a kiss and heads out.

Paloma takes the chair and says, "If you really want to learn Spanish, Luna, you should join the mariachi group. It's open to ages ten and up."

"But if I can't *speak* Spanish, how will I ever *sing* it?"

"It's actually easier to sing. Most opera singers do entire performances in languages they don't speak. The melody helps you remember the words. That's why we sing the alphabet instead of speaking it."

I'd never thought about that before, but it makes sense.

"Just think about it," Paloma says. "You can take beginner classes. That's what *I* did. They're at the Antonio Garcia Arts Center on Agnes Street."

"I don't know," I say. "Maybe."

"I have a performance next week. You should come. I'll introduce you to everybody. They're very nice. Invite the other primas so we can all be friends again. Except ... maybe not Claudia. Mirasol's mad at her because Claudia found out that she was driving her friend's car. My sis turns fifteen and thinks she can do everything, even drive. I don't know how Claudia found out, but she did and she tattled and now Mirasol is grounded."

We talk a little more before hanging up. Then I call Marina, Estrella, and Celeste. I tell them that Paloma and I made up and that it was all a misunderstanding. She didn't mean to embarrass me, and she *did* give me the correct definition for "cama."

My cousins say that if I forgive Paloma, then they forgive her, too. Marina's not going to unfriend her, Celeste isn't going to break the Snapchat streak, and Estrella's not going to take back the cell phone cover.

So all the Ramos primas are friends again. Well, *almost* all, because some of us are still mad at Claudia.

Hablar

When I see Claudia the next morning, she's at the table, but instead of eating, she's knitting. I don't talk to her and she doesn't talk to me. She's probably still mad about the flies, and I'm *definitely* mad about the gossip.

Mom notices, so she tries to start a conversation. "What are you making, Claudia?"

Claudia glances at me and says, "It's a surprise." She holds up her knitting project. "I had to start over because I want it to be perfect." Sure enough, the blob is gone. She's got a circle now. It's the size of a coaster.

"You should join the knitting club with Claudia," Mom tells me. "You need some extracurricular activities, and it'll give you a chance to be with your prima."

Spending more time with Claudia is the last thing I need, so I say, "I signed up for Community Gardeners." I reach in my backpack and hand over the supply list. "And Paloma says I should join the mariachi group, too.

She invited me to one of her performances so I could meet everyone."

I glance at Claudia, and she glances back but quickly turns away. I can tell she's jealous because Paloma invited me and not her, but Claudia doesn't say anything. She just keeps knitting.

When Claudia and I walk to the bus stop, we don't talk, and when we get on the bus, we still don't talk. If only the other kids could be quiet, too, but they can't. They say "Cruella de Vil" again, and a few kids hold their noses.

I settle into my seat. "I'm getting tired of this," I tell Mabel. "They're still making jokes about Claudia's nose and my hair. I have two and a half weeks before I can wear hats again. I wish I never locked my cousin in the bathroom. Why didn't you stop me?"

"I tried," she says, and sighs. "But you were being stubborn."

I glance back at Claudia. She does not look happy, either. I'm sure she's tired of the jokes, too. Instead of hiding behind a book, she's hiding behind her knitting, and her needles lightly tap as she works on that green circle.

"Aren't they getting bored?" I say about the kids who keep teasing. "Can't they talk about something else?"

"Why don't *we* talk about something else?" Mabel suggests.

"You mean ignore them?"

"Yeah. Sometimes when I want to ignore something, I daydream. I think about something nice like riding a horse on the beach." She closes her eyes. "We're running and his hooves kick up the sand. All I can hear is the wind." She smiles, and then she just sits there, lost in her daydream.

I snap a few times. "Earth to Mabel. Come back to reality."

She opens her eyes. "Now you try it. Tune out these kids. See if you can escape by pretending you're riding a horse on the beach."

It's a silly idea, but I decide to try. Who knows? Maybe daydreaming is better than drinking lots of water and squeezing starfish.

I close my eyes. I'm on Padre Island, early in the morning before lots of people have arrived. I'm on a horse. It's brown with a black mane, and it smells like a dog that hasn't taken a bath for a very long time. I'm wearing boots and a cowboy hat because this is Texas and that's what you wear when you ride horses. I say "Giddyup." The horse takes a few steps. I say "Giddyup!" again, this time louder. The horse speeds up. Soon, we're running, faster and faster, and Mabel's right—I can feel the wind in my face. Instead of jokes, I hear waves. I'm strong, free, and happy, but then my cowboy hat flies off and seagulls start chasing me, dipping down as if to peck me.

They're going "Caw, caw, caw," but all I hear is "Ha, ha, ha"—like they're laughing—laughing at my hair!

I open my eyes.

"See?" Mabel says. "Don't you feel better?"

I nod, but I'm squeezing the starfish. When I get to school, I rush to the water fountain and drink enough to fill two bottles. I don't care how many times I go to the restroom.

And Claudia doesn't care how much she knits. Before class starts, she sits in her desk, her needles going tap, tap, tap. She knits during recess, too, and after she finishes lunch, she knits again. Then school's over, and she knits on the bus ride home. Every time kids pinch their noses, say it stinks, or make up silly rhymes, Claudia gives them an angry look and starts knitting. I can tell she's getting tired when she rests her hands, but then she opens and closes her fists as if to stretch her fingers, and after that, starts knitting again. I don't know what she's making, but little by little, the green circle is growing. Soon it's the size of a small plate.

After watching my prima knit for two more days, I ask my dad a question. "Why does Claudia knit when kids make fun of her nose?"

"Why are they making fun of her nose?" he asks.

"Because it's big."

"It is?"

"Dad, it *enormous*!"

"Hmmm . . . I never noticed, but you know me. I wouldn't notice a carousel if it were spinning in our front yard." He laughs at himself.

"So why does Claudia knit all the time?" I ask again.

"It's probably a coping mechanism."

"Coping mechanism? What's that?"

"Something you do when you're feeling stressed out. It's supposed to help you relax. Like taking a long walk or petting a dog."

"Dogs bark a lot," I say. "It's probably more relaxing to pet a rabbit."

"Maybe," he says. "We all have different ways of dealing with stress. For example, your mom likes to shop with her sisters and I like to watch *Star Trek* reruns."

I nod because Abuela and Mom's advice makes perfect sense now. They were giving me coping mechanisms when they told me to drink water or squeeze a spongy starfish. Mabel's daydream was a coping mechanism, too. I guess I could also try shopping, watching reruns, knitting, and anything else that will help me forget my problems, and if I wait long enough, like two and a half more weeks when I can wear hats again, then maybe my problems will finally go away.

El desayuno

It's Friday morning and Claudia's here for breakfast. With a mouth full of waffles, she asks me, "Did you do your homework?"

"Yes. Not that it's any of your business."

"All of it?" She glances at my mom as she says this.

I hate to lie but I also hate to admit that I didn't do all my homework, because after eating dinner, playing LEGOs with Alex, watching "Funny Bunny" videos on YouTube, and cutting out pictures from old magazines, I ran out of time.

"The math problems *and* the spelling words," Claudia adds because I haven't answered.

"Lucky Luna," Mom says, "did you do your math problems? I didn't see you do any math."

"No, but I copied my spelling words three times. It took forever, so I didn't have a chance to do anything else."

That should settle it, but Claudia wants me to get in trouble. "How about Spanish? Did you practice Spanish? You don't want to get another F, do you?"

"We didn't have Spanish homework," I say.

"But maybe your parents can give you extra lessons," she suggests. "That way, you can learn more words with the correct definitions." She turns to my mom. "Did you know that Luna thought 'cama' meant 'canal'?"

Mom raises an eyebrow, questioning me.

"I know what it really means," I say. "It means 'bed.'"

Mom sighs with relief. "That's right, mija. But maybe we can practice Spanish this weekend. I need to improve, too, so maybe your dad can help us both."

Claudia smiles. I can tell she's happy about giving me work over the weekend, so while we're waiting for the bus, I say, "You are not my teacher. Stop making extra homework assignments."

"I'm just trying to help."

"You are not helping. You are stressing me out. I already have a bunch of homework and chores without your extra ideas. Last night I had to do spelling, math, and reading." Since that doesn't seem like a long list, I add a few more tasks. "I also had to wash dishes, fold towels, dust the living room furniture, and give Alex a bath. I don't have time for anything else. I'm already exhausted. Look at how exhausted I am." I yawn to make my point. I didn't really do all these things last night, but it's not a lie because I'll probably do them over the weekend.

"That is a fake yawn."

"No, it isn't."

"Yes, it is, Luna. I can tell the difference between a fake yawn and a real one."

I glare at her. If she's going to get on my nerves, then I'm going to get on hers. "You think you know everything," I say, "but I know a few things, too, like why our primas ignore you sometimes."

"No, they don't. *I* got to stand in the quinceañera, remember?"

"Only because you're one month older and Mirasol didn't want it to look like she was picking favorites."

"You're not her favorite."

"How many times has she painted *your* nails?"

She looks at her fingernails. They aren't painted. They don't even have a clear coat.

"Just admit it," I say. "When you talk to our primas, it's because *you* call *them*, not because *they* call *you*."

She gets a hurt look on her face, and she doesn't have a comeback, probably for the first time in her entire life. That means I hit a sore spot. I meant to, but instead of feeling happy about getting revenge, I feel miserable. I thought my punch would be like a hard pat, not like a bone-crushing blow to the ribs. Claudia's still silent, which makes me think about *my* silence when kids make old-person jokes about my hair.

We get on the bus, and I sit beside Mabel and glance back to make sure Claudia isn't crying about being ignored by our primas. But she isn't. She isn't crying, and she isn't in her regular seat. She's behind Janie and Carly, my mortal enemies! I thought they were her mortal enemies, too, but I guess not. She's talking to them, all friendly. They're laughing about something. I can't hear what they're saying, but they're probably laughing about me.

I can't believe I felt sorry for my prima and almost apologized. She might be my cousin, but she is *not* my friend.

Mabel is my friend. She's the best friend in the whole, wide world. As soon as we get to school, she grabs my hand and pulls me to the building.

"Where are you taking me?"

"To the club board."

I learn why she's excited when we get there. The Woodlawn newsletter is ready. Mabel checks to see if the new edition is posted on the bulletin board. It is, and she points to her name because she's listed as one of the reporters. Instead of reading it in the hallway, we hurry to class.

"Let's see if Mr. Cruz has copies," she says. But we don't have to ask because he's handing them out as we enter.

We get to our desks and start reading. There's a "study tip" section about reading aloud, a "kudos" section about Dylan Moore, who won the spelling bee, a "club corner" section with updates from different clubs, and a "save the date" section with announcements about Family Night and the Woodlawn Talent Show. But Mabel's not interested in any of that. She wants me to read the "spotlight" section because it has a picture of Claudia and the paragraph that Mabel wrote.

> *Woodlawn Elementary welcomes fifth grader Claudia Salazar. She spent first through fourth grades at Sacred Heart Catholic School but switched to our campus because of our wonderful after-school activities. So far, she has joined Needle Beetles, and she plans to join a few more clubs next month. Her hobbies are playing the ukulele and reading. Her favorite color is blue. Claudia is very friendly, and we are lucky to have her in our school.*

Since when is Claudia's favorite color blue? If she likes blue so much, then why is she knitting something green? That's *my* favorite color—except that *I* like green like parrot feathers, not green like moldy cheese. Plus, Mabel wrote nothing about Claudia showing off and tattling every chance she gets. And there's nothing about Claudia acting like a teacher's pet by volunteering to pass out worksheets or being bossy by telling everyone what they should or shouldn't eat for lunch. And there's absolutely nothing about Claudia's giant nose, not even in the picture. It was probably photoshopped so her nose would seem normal.

"Well?" Mabel asks. "What do you think? Do you like my profile?"

There's only one right answer because Mabel's my best friend. "It's very nice," I say. I don't *think* it, but I *say* it because lying to make someone happy is sometimes better than telling the truth.

Then Nick, another student in the class, comes up and says, "Good job on the newsletter, Mabel." He glances at me and smirks before adding, "I have an idea. You should add a section called 'freak show' and write articles about the weird people at our school." He doesn't say anything else, but he nods in my direction.

I can't help it. I've had enough. I'm not ashamed anymore. I'm outright mad! And anger speaks . . . no, it yells! "Stop making jokes about my hair!"

Everyone freezes and looks at me. I've been singled out in the worst way.

I rush toward the door. As I pass Claudia, she grabs my shoulder and asks if I'm okay. I shrug her off. John-John's entering the room, and I almost bump into him. "Where are you going?" he asks, but I don't answer.

Once I get to the hall, I run to the restroom. Some girls are in there, but I ignore them and find an empty stall where I can hide.

I know I'll have to return to class soon, but for now, the restroom stall feels like the safest place because the only thing people can see are my feet, which aren't too big or too small and which have ten toes, no extras—but even if they *did* have extras, no one would notice because I'm wearing tennis shoes, the same type that everybody else wears. My feet do not belong in a "freak show" section of a newsletter because they're the most normal feet in the world. If only I had the most normal hair, too.

El fin de semana

During the weekend, I ask Mom if I can start wearing hats again. I ask three times, and three times she says no. I'm facing two more weeks of torture. When I tell Mom about the teasing, she reminds me that I have "lovely hair and shouldn't hide it." Well, that's easy for her to say. She has brown hair with zero white strands, but even if she *did* have white strands, no one would comment because she's already old.

On Sunday, my dad and I watch a rerun of *Star Trek: The Next Generation*. In the episode, the crew starts the day by playing poker but then their ship explodes and they all die. The events repeat over and over but no one remembers except Dr. Crusher, who begins to see clues. Little by little, they solve the mystery. Turns out, they're in a time loop.

I feel like I'm in a time loop, too, because soon it's Monday again. Claudia's in the kitchen like before, and she's eating the only banana that doesn't have black spots. She's still knitting, and on the bus, kids are still holding their noses.

But this is where things change, because instead of hiding in her seat, Claudia stands in the middle of the aisle, hands on hips. "I'm sick and tired of seeing you grab your noses when we get on the bus. Grow up, people!" The nostrils of her giant nose open wide as she huffs and puffs like the Big Bad Wolf. She actually scares the little ones. They stop pinching their noses and try hiding in their seats.

Claudia *still* looks like the Big Bad Wolf when we get to the classroom. Mr. Cruz notices. "Is everything okay, Claudia?"

"No," my prima answers. "But I'm taking care of it."

"Hmmm . . ." he mutters. Then, to the rest of us, he says, "I hope we aren't having issues in this class, but if we are, please come talk to me."

He gives us a moment to think about it and tells us to get ready for mini bees. That's when we practice spelling words with our friends. I always practice with Mabel and John-John.

I get the first word, "description." This week, we're doing words that end in "t-i-o-n." They should end in "s-h-u-n" because that's how they sound, but if there's one thing I've learned about English, you can't always spell by sound. After I spell it, I say, "Looks like Claudia finally got tired of hearing jokes about her nose."

Mabel and John-John glance at each other. Then Mabel says, "Maybe they weren't talking about her nose."

"What do you mean?" I ask. "Why else would they say it stinks?"

"There could be lots of reasons," she says.

I nod toward John-John. "Yeah, like throwing up worms and grilled cheese sandwiches?"

Mabel and John-John glance at each other again, but they don't say anything. Instead, we move on to the next spelling word.

During recess, Mabel and I find a shady tree, but rather than sit on a bench with her new friends, Claudia marches to the middle of the playground.

"Listen up, people!" And they *do* listen because it sounds as if she has a megaphone. "I have an announcement." She holds up a knitting needle. It looks like a little sword. "Nobody's perfect. All of us have something that makes us different, but that doesn't mean we're weird. It just means that we're unique, which is a cool thing if you ask me. That's why we should accept people for who they are and not for how they look."

Some kids look down because they've been rude, but others give Claudia a thumbs-up—like Harold with the bushy eyebrows and Lucy with the chapped lips. They get teased, too. There's a lot of teasing at my school. Sometimes I forget that other kids are having a hard time, because I'm too focused on my own problems.

After her big announcement, Claudia heads our way and sits under our tree. "There's plenty of shade here," she says, "so don't tell me to leave." And she starts knitting again. I still don't know what she's making. It looks like a bowl but not for cereal because the milk would seep through.

When we return to class, Claudia changes her seat. She tells John-John, "Switch with me. Just for today." He mumbles but moves anyway.

I whisper, "Stop spying on me."

She whispers back, "I'm not."

I don't believe her, so when we get a worksheet, I hunch over and try to block her view. I write itsy-bitsy letters so she can't read my answers. But hunching over is a bad idea because my neck and shoulders start to hurt and a headache starts to form because I'm squinting.

I forgot the starfish today, so I try Mabel's coping mechanism by daydreaming about a horse. But instead of a sunny beach, there's a storm, and the harsh winds are throwing sand in my mouth and eyes. I can't see, and I can barely breathe. Mabel's daydream is making things worse, not better. If only I had a rabbit. A rabbit would calm me down a lot more than a horse.

Then it's time for lunch. Claudia dumps her new friends again and comes to my table.

"Quit following me," I say. "Quit *spying*."

"That's not what I'm doing. I'm here to protect you.

Trust me, no one's going to say you stink when I'm around."

Did I hear right? I shake my head for a double take and turn to Mabel. "Are people saying I stink?"

She shrugs.

"But I have a normal-sized nose," I say.

Mabel looks down. I can tell she doesn't want to answer, but after a moment, she finally says something. "They're not making fun of your nose, Luna. They're making fun of your hair."

"Of course they're making fun of my hair! I've been hearing old-person jokes all week. But that doesn't mean I smell bad."

She takes a deep breath. She looks like someone who's about to swallow the worst-tasting medicine. "They're saying you look like a skunk."

I do another double take. So not only am I prematurely old but I'm a stinky mammal, too.

"Why didn't you tell me?" I ask Mabel.

Claudia answers instead. "How could you *not* know?"

"It seems obvious now," I say, "but I really didn't. Whenever I heard a skunk comment or saw kids holding their noses, I thought it was because of John-John throwing up or because they were making fun of *you*."

"Of *me*?" Claudia's surprised. "Why would they make fun of me?"

"Because of your giant nose."

"I do *not* have a giant nose."

"She doesn't," Mabel agrees. "I've been trying to tell you. Claudia's nose is normal."

"In fact," Claudia says, "if I have a big nose, then so do you because even though our hair is different and our eyes are different and our lips are different, our noses are exactly the same."

To prove it, she reaches in her purse and takes out a compact mirror. I take it and look at my nose, then at hers, and then at mine again. I can't believe it. Our noses are exactly the same! Claudia and Mabel are right. Why didn't I see it before?

I hand back the mirror. "So we have the same nose," I admit. "I wish we had the same hair instead, because then I wouldn't have this birthmark."

"We can't always get what we wish," Claudia replies. "Now, stop separating your carrots and peas. You should eat *all* your vegetables. If you don't, I'm telling your mom."

Mabel tugs my sleeve. "I like your white hair. It makes you unique just like Claudia said at recess. Look, I have a birthmark, too." She rolls down her sock and shows me a brown splotch on her ankle.

I'm glad she reminded me about her birthmark, but a splotch beneath a sock is not the same as a streak of white hair. Sometimes being unique is a good-luck thing like when you're the fastest runner, the best dancer, or the only person in class who knows how to make home-made ice cream. But when it comes to uniqueness, I have the bad-luck kind.

After school, we get on the bus. Claudia, too.

"Don't you have Needle Beetles?" I ask.

"I'm skipping it today." Then, instead of three rows behind, she sits one row in front of Mabel and me. "It's only for today," she says, just like when she made John-John move. "I don't *actually* want to sit here."

She faces the front of the bus and starts knitting again. I can hear the needles clinking. For the first time since I locked Claudia in the restroom and got grounded from wearing hats, no one holds their nose or says it stinks or makes an old-person joke. I'm sure they still want to, but they're too afraid of my prima.

We're almost to Mabel's stop, when Claudia turns around, hands me the green thing she's been knitting, and says, "Finally. The answer to all your problems."

La respuesta

Claudia's respuesta makes no sense. How is this green thingamajig the answer to my problems when I have no idea what it is?

"Don't you like it?" Claudia asks. "Isn't green your favorite color?"

"Yes," I say, even though I like Kermit-the-Frog and not snot-and-boogers green.

"Then what's wrong? I've been knitting twenty-four/seven for a whole week! I had to start over three times to make it perfect. I even got a blister." She holds up a finger, and sure enough, there's a blister.

She was doing something nice, so I try to be polite. "Thanks, Claudia. I'm sure this bowl will come in handy when I eat Cheetos."

Mabel giggles. "That's not a bowl." She takes it from me and fits it over my head. "It's a hat." We're at her stop, so she grabs her things. Before she leaves, she turns to Claudia. "Will you teach me how to knit? I want to make hats, too."

"Sure," Claudia says. "Knitting's fun."

Mabel thanks her, and then she's off the bus.

I look at my reflection in the window, tucking away most of my white hair. The hat fits perfectly. I touch the soft yarn and smile. I want to be happy, but I can't help feeling suspicious.

I tap Claudia on the shoulder. "I thought you didn't like me. You're not trying to get me in trouble by giving me a hat when you know I'm not supposed to wear one, are you?"

"No. This can be our secret. I promise not to tell."

"Really? Why are you being nice? Why did you make all those announcements today and tell the kids to leave me alone?"

She takes a moment to speak. "At first, I didn't care if people made fun of you because I was still mad about getting locked in the restroom. In my opinion, you deserved to be teased. But then it didn't stop, and all those people started getting on my nerves. I kept wondering . . . didn't they have anything better to talk about? How many times can they repeat stuff about your hair? All those jokes got old on day two." She shakes her head with disbelief. Then she says, "When you got upset in class the other day and ran out, that was it. I got mad—not *at* you, but *for* you. Like they say, 'La sangre es más espesa que el agua.'"

Wait a minute! I think. *She just repeated Abuela, word for word!*

"Abuela told me the same thing about agua. Is that a dicho or something?"

Claudia pauses before answering. "It's an English proverb, but I'm not sure it translates to Spanish exactly. When we were at the quinceañera, I was complaining about having to go to your school. I knew you would cause all kinds of trouble."

I think back and remember seeing Claudia with her mom and Abuela, all glancing in my direction. I thought I was being paranoid, that they were *really* looking at someone else, but I guess they were talking about *me* after all.

"So Abuela told you to drink water as a coping mechanism?"

Claudia looks at me, confused. "No. Why would she say that?"

"Isn't that what 'la sangre, blah, blah, agua' means?"

She laughs, and I feel like the dumbest person in the world. "So *that's* why you were drinking so much water? This is hilarious. I can't wait to tell our primas and your mom so she can see why you need extra Spanish lessons."

I want to scream, but I hold it in. Still, I have to ask, "Why do you have to be such a tattle all the time?"

"I am *not* tattling," Claudia says, offended. "I'm *informing*."

The bus reaches our stop, so Claudia and I make our exit. Instead of heading home, we stay at the corner, facing off.

"Well, your 'informing'"—I put air quotes around the word—"gets me in trouble. It gets our primas in trouble, too. Remember when I said they don't like you around?"

She crosses her arms. She'll make a great prison guard someday.

"I wasn't trying to be mean," I say. "Well . . . I *was* . . . but I was also telling the truth. We can't do or say anything without you telling our parents and getting us in trouble. Who wants to be in trouble all the time? It's better to keep you out of the loop."

Suddenly, Claudia doesn't look like a prison guard anymore. She looks like a regular fifth grader whose feelings are hurt. "I'm not trying to get you guys in trouble," she says. "I'm trying to help you."

"How does tattling help us?"

"Because . . ." She takes a moment. "I tell your mom about your grades so you can do better in school, and I tell her about how you don't eat your veggies so you can get good nutrition."

"And Mirasol driving with her friends? You tattled about that, too."

"She doesn't have a license yet. She could get a ticket, or worse, get in an accident!"

"And how about Celeste kissing her boyfriend in the parking lot at the quinceañera?"

"She shouldn't be kissing in public like that. It could ruin her reputation!"

"That's so old-fashioned," I say. Then I give her more examples of tattling, and for each one, she has an explanation. She totally believes that she's doing it for our own good, and all of the sudden, I'm starting to believe it, too. When Claudia tattles, she's not being mean on purpose. I thought she was trying to get us in trouble, but in her mind, she's helping us.

I put a hand on her shoulder. "I didn't know you were tattling for those reasons and that you just wanted me to be healthy, smart, and bilingual." I pause because I can't believe what I'm about to say. "Thanks, prima. Thanks for looking out for me."

And then I realize something else. Not once did Claudia make jokes about my hair or laugh at me. And today, she stood up to those bullies. She was helping me, so now it's *my* turn to help *her*.

"I don't think our primas are going to understand why you tell on them," I say. "They like to focus on the negative and forget the positive, if you know what I mean."

She nods. "I do. They're very stubborn."

"Exactly."

She thinks a moment. "I can't stop informing about the big things like driving without a license because my primas could get seriously hurt. I couldn't live with myself if that happened. But I could stop telling about the small things even if it means they'll get in trouble—maybe not with their parents but in other ways."

"At least they won't blame you for it."

"That's true."

I decide to take a risk. It means helping Claudia by going behind Paloma's back, but it's for a good cause. Besides, I owe Claudia because she stood up for me and made me a hat. Maybe it's an ugly version of green but at least it's soft.

"Why don't you come to Paloma's mariachi performance?" I say. "It's on Thursday. You can ride with me and we can sit together. Maybe you can translate the songs, and if you start to tattle about something, I'll give you a signal—like tugging my ear. That way, you can stop yourself before it's too late. Once our primas see that you aren't a tattletale anymore, they'll start calling and inviting you places."

She thinks about it. "You really want me to go? Even though Paloma didn't invite me herself?"

"Sure," I say. "She won't turn you away once you're there. She'll probably be glad to see you. Especially if you clap and throw out some gritos."

Claudia smiles. Then she says, "I guess what my mom and Abuela said about la sangre y agua is true."

I scratch my head. "Yeah, about that. I still don't know what it means."

"Well, it's not about drinking water," Claudia laughs. Then she gets serious. "It means 'blood is thicker than water.' My mom said it first because it's an English dicho, if there's such a thing. Then Abuela asked her to translate because she doesn't understand English very well."

Hmmm . . . I think. *Blood is thicker than water.* I repeat it several times as I try to understand. When I remember what Dad said about the moscas and how you can't always take things word for word, I try to figure out what blood symbolizes. The only thing I can think of is this: Claudia and I have the same blood because we have the same grandparents and the same nose, so nothing, not even our biggest, meanest fight, can keep us from being a part of the same family.

La familia

The next Thursday, Claudia joins my family for Paloma's mariachi concert at the Antonio E. Garcia Arts & Education Center. We walk into a bright room. Along one wall are paintings of Mexican children doing different things like playing baseball, eating snow cones, or climbing trees. On another wall is a huge mural featuring horses and cowboys. There are also rows of chairs and a platform for the stage, and along the back, a long table with pan dulces.

Lots of voices echo in the room, and I can easily pick out the sounds of my primas. Many of them are here— Mirasol, of course, since she's Paloma's sister, and Josie, Kimberly, Celeste, Estrella, and Marina. They're already sitting, and they've placed purses and sweaters on a second row to save chairs for the rest of us.

"Primas!" I say as I take a seat behind them.

They turn around. "Prima!" they say back. Then they spot Claudia. Everyone says hello, but not Mirasol or Celeste because they're still mad about the tattling. When they turn away from her, Claudia rolls her eyes, more irritated than hurt.

I tap my cousins' shoulders. "Claudia has something to say," I tell them when they turn again.

"I do?" Claudia asks.

"Yes. Remember? About the tattling. You wanted to apologize."

She takes a deep breath because saying "I'm sorry" is like admitting you're wrong, and Claudia would rather eat earthworms with John-John than admit being wrong.

"Well . . . I just want to say," she begins, "I wasn't trying to get you in trouble. I was trying to protect you." And she goes on, telling them what she told me about the reasons for all her tattling. Celeste and Mirasol cross their arms. "Uh-huh," "Oh yeah," and "Really," they mutter.

"It's no fun being stuck at home for a whole month," Mirasol says.

"The only reason I'm here," Celeste adds, "is because it's a family outing, and that's the only kind of outing I can have."

When she says this, Mirasol shifts her attention. "Wait

a minute," she tells Celeste, "I thought you were here to support my sister."

Celeste shrugs. "I am . . . sort of . . . but . . . I don't even like mariachi music."

Then Kimberly and Josie jump in, shocked that Celeste hates mariachi music, and Marina and Estrella have an opinion, too, saying that it's not about the music at all but about Paloma. Soon, there's a lot of bickering back and forth, and I can't believe it—my primas are about to erupt into a major argument seconds before Paloma's group takes the stage.

"See?" Claudia tells me as she nods toward my squabbling primas. "They can always find a reason to be mad." She leans back in her chair, smug. This is her way of telling me that she was right all along—it was useless to apologize.

I can't help agreeing with Claudia as I try to follow my cousins' arguments. They aren't talking about whether or not they like mariachi music anymore. They've moved on to stuff that happened months ago—like the time Josie flirted with Celeste's boyfriend, and the time Marina's dog chewed up Estrella's favorite emoji pillow, and the time one of Nancy's science experiments burned a hole in Aunt Priscilla's favorite apron. Nancy and Aunt Priscilla aren't even here, but they still get pulled into the argument. And everyone takes sides. First, Estrella and Marina are together, then Josie and

Kimberly, then Kimberly and Estrella—my primas teaming up one minute and splitting apart the next.

Then Abuela shows up. My parents, aunts, and uncles stand behind her, making Abuela seem like a general of an army. She puts two fingers in her mouth and whistles to get our attention. All my primas go silent.

"Mijas, por favor," Abuela says. "¿Por qué hacen tanto ruido? Esta es una ocasión especial. Estamos aquí por Paloma." She pauses, making sure to look at each of us directly. "Una familia amable para ella. ¿Me entienden?"

She takes a minute to let her wise words sink in. Of course, I don't understand what she said, but I know enough to nod when I hear "entienden." My primas nod, too. A few mutter apologies—not to each other but to Abuela. The last thing we want is to embarrass her.

When Abuela is satisfied, she and our parents take their seats, my large familia needing two full rows. Soon the lights blink off and on, letting the audience know that the show is about to begin.

We hear the mariachi group before we see them— guitars, violins, and trumpets. Then they come in through a side door. There are six people in the group— four boys and two girls. All are wearing black charro outfits with wide red bow ties and sombreros. They're singing "Guadalajara," the same song Paloma practiced when I visited her house for the fish fry. Her hands flutter over the strings, and when she holds a note, she closes her eyes. I can tell that she is putting her heart and soul into the music. One of the singers gestures to us so we can join in. Many in the crowd know the words, and even though I don't, I hum along. All of a sudden, Abuela utters a grito, a loud celebratory shout. She taps my primas in the front row, encouraging them to shout gritos, too. Estrella tries, but hers is short and sharp like the sound a dog makes when you step on its tail. Marina tries next, and it's better but not loud enough.

Then Claudia stands up, cups her hands over her mouth, and shouts, "Hai-yai-yai-yaaaaaaaaai!" It's the most heartfelt grito I've ever heard. Paloma beams with pride, and the other mariachis nod in appreciation.

Celeste offers a fist bump and says, "Way to go, prima!" And Mirasol says, "You've got a great pair of lungs!"

Claudia sits back down, a triumphant smile on her face. That's when I realize that even though Celeste and Mirasol haven't officially accepted Claudia's apology, they have forgiven her for all the tattling. In fact, we all have forgiven one another for the times we made mistakes or did mean things on purpose, because it's too hard to stay mad when one of our primas is playing the guitar and making us proud.

The song ends. We clap and together we ask for an encore. "¡Otra! ¡Otra! ¡Otra!" we chant.

The music starts again. This time they're playing "Cielito Lindo." I actually know one of the lines. It goes, "Ay, ay, ay, ay. Canta y no llores," and it means, "Ay, ay, ay, ay. Sing and don't cry," the perfect words for my family right now because instead of crying and complaining, we're singing and cheering.

My parents, Abuela, my aunts, my uncles, and especially my primas—all of us are swaying and tapping our feet to the rhythm, keeping perfect time with the music and with one another. That's what "blood is thicker than water" *really* means. It's not about having the same noses or hair color or grandparents. It's about having the same hearts. My primas may bicker, compete, gossip, and tattle, but they'll always be my primas no matter what . . . and having lots of primas is a very good-luck thing.

Glossary of Chapter Titles

1. La prima—girl cousin

2. Olvidar—to forget

3. El chisme—gossip

4. El Domingo—Sunday

5. La luna—moon

6. La cocina—kitchen

7. La abuela—grandmother

8. ¿Dónde está?—where is

9. La amiga—girl friend

10. La semana—week

11. Enojado—angry

12. Ándale—hurry

13. La guitarra—guitar

14. Otra vez—again

15. Buenos días—good morning

16. El problema—problem

17. El nombre—name

18. Las moscas—flies (as in insects)

19. La galleta—cookie

20. La noche—night

21. Hablar—to talk

22. El desayuno—breakfast

23. El fin de semana—weekend

24. La respuesta—an answer

25. La familia—family

Acknowledgments

I'm blessed with many people who support and encourage me. I'd like to thank Stefanie Von Borstel, my wonderful agent and friend. Much gratitude also goes to Nancy Mercado and the entire team at Scholastic. Mom, Dad, Albert, Tricia, Steven, y todos mis sobrinos continue to inspire me. My husband, Gene, and friends Vanesa, Saba, and San Juan continue to patiently listen as I blab about book ideas. And finally, a shout-out to mis primas. Like Luna, I have too many to count, but all are unique and loved.

About the Author

Diana López is the award-winning author of *Ask My Mood Ring How I Feel*, *Confetti Girl*, and *Nothing Up My Sleeve*, among others. Beyond that, she is also the editor of the literary magazine *Huizache* and the managing director of CentroVictoria, an organization devoted to promoting Mexican American literature. She lives in South Texas and teaches at the University of Houston–Victoria. She also has several primas . . . whom she gets along with most of the time.